frustration and lust
the year' Gill Paul

'Every page contains
don't follow the cha............ ... . alongside
them, turning the pages in an ever-increasing
frenzy' Jean-Paul Delfino

'Enchanting, beautiful, poetic … This novel creates
the most indescribable feelings in readers' Babelio

'Spellbinding, disconcerting and hypnotic … an
amalgamation of Shakespearean tragedy, the spirit
of Lewis Carroll and the vivid descriptions of
Wuthering Heights' Aurélie Dye-Pellisson

'Anne Sénès offers us a "double room" in which
"perfumes, colours and sounds respond to one
another" in the manner of Baudelaire. Poetic and so
close to reality!'
Marie Theron, Librairie Charlemagne

'Interesting and beautiful … a unique read'
Independent Book Reviews

About The Author

Anne Sénès was born in Paris and studied at the Sorbonne, where she obtained a PhD in English studies. Her passion for Anglo-Saxon literature and culture has taken her all over the world, from London to Miami, passing through the south of France. She is currently based on the Mediterranean coast, where she works as a journalist and translator. *Double Room* is her first literary novel.

Follow Anne on Instagram, @anne_senes83

About The Translator

Alice Banks was born in Shropshire and completed her MA in Literary Translation at the University of East Anglia. She now lives in Madrid, where she works as a translator from French and Spanish into English. Her first translation, *Deranged As I Am*, by Comoros writer, Ali Zamir, was published in 2022 and was followed by *Madrid Will Be Their Tomb*, by Elizabeth Duval, published in 2023.

Alice collaborates with Hablemos, escritoras to translate their podcasts and content into English, and also with the European Literature Network, where she worked as Assistant Editor on the Spanish edition of *The Riveter* magazine.

Praise For *Double Room*

'A masterful exploration of vulnerability, shifting memory and loss. Anne Sénès writes with sharp yet tender insight. Her words contain a subtle urgency that keep the pages turning. *Double Room* is a book that will linger long after the final page. It will haunt you with what is said and what is left unsaid. It is simply brilliant' Jill Johnson

'Told in an achingly beautiful voice, *Double Room* drew me into a world full of mystery, music and bittersweet love, and wouldn't let me go. Every sentence is poetic, every page is captivating. I could not stop reading but knew I had to slow down for fear of it being over too soon. Sénès, and her translator, Alice Banks, have a gift for bringing characters and places alive with astute observations of the tiniest details. I could picture, taste and smell every scene. A masterful translation of a stunning novel, *Double Room* is everything I want in a story and more – exquisitely written, populated with fascinating characters and full of surprises' Katie Allen

'This spellbinding novel takes readers on a multi-sensory journey through love and loss, grief,

Double Room

Anne Sénès

Translated by Alice Banks

**ORENDA
BOOKS**

Orenda Books
16 Carson Road
West Dulwich
London SE21 8HU
www.orendabooks.co.uk

First published in the United Kingdom by Orenda Books, 2025
First published in French as *Chambre Double* by Le bruit du monde, 2023
Chambre double Copyright © Anne Sénès, 2023
By agreement with Pontas Literary & Film Agency
English translation copyright © Alice Banks, 2025
The translator was kindly supported by the Society of Authors Authors'
Foundation Grant for the duration of her work on this translation.

A catalogue record for this book is available from the British Library.

ISBN 978-1-916788-56-5
eISBN 978-1-916788-57-2

Typeset in Charter by typesetter.org.uk
Printed and bound by Clays Ltd, Elcograf S.p.A

For sales and distribution, please contact info@orendabooks.co.uk
or visit *www.orendabooks.co.uk.*

For Thomas,
my link between France and England.

'Here everything has the adequate clarity
of harmony's delicious obscurity.'

Charles Baudelaire, *The Double Room*,
tr. Walker Evans [1]

---
[1] https://www.metmuseum.org/art/collection/search/283741

'Are you listening? Stan? Hello? Stan? Are you asleep?'

Asleep? How could I be asleep, when for almost twenty minutes, for what seems to me a lifetime, Babette has been soliloquising. We've said everything there is to say. We've discussed it all. My silences, my lack of involvement in our life together, my voluntary confinement, my refusal to go out more often. Stan. Stan. Stan.

Babette. Babette. Babette. Whose swimming costumes exude the scent of chlorine, which slowly permeates the walls of the house – the Rabbit Hole, as Lisa has always called it. Whose tofu- and grain-based recipes with names that are impossible to recall brighten up our day-to-day. Whose son, Téo, lives tethered to his iPhone like a suffering, shipwrecked sailor to his raft.

I sigh. 'Listen, Bab, I know it's difficult.' And then, with no little hypocrisy, I add, 'Especially for you, but…'

Now it's Babette's turn to sigh, 'I know, I know…'

There's no need to allude verbally to Liv's death for the colours of grief to flood our bedroom. Nor to mention that Lisa has lost her mother. There's nothing Babette can do. There's nothing I can do. There's nothing Lisa can do. We have to live with it – that's just the way it is. Usually, I only have to hint at the possibility of taking the discussion in that direction and Babette gives up the pursuit. Not this evening, though. She's back on the offensive:

'…but the fact remains, Stan, that this can't go on. Téo and I, we're not second-class citizens in this methodical little life you've built around yourself. We need – I need – to find my place within this household. I admit that sometimes I can be a bit heavy-handed, that I'm partly to blame, but if you don't take responsibility…'

It's time to sleep, hums Laïvely, our automated home assistant, before abruptly switching off the lamp on my bedside table.

Babette's body tenses at my side. I hold my breath.

It's time to sleep, had resonated in more vermillion tones than usual. Was Laïvely losing her patience too?

London

TWENTY YEARS EARLIER

It was her laughter I discovered first. A tinkling tune with yellowed edges and a touch of taupe at the seams. Something I had never heard, never felt before.

Only her back was visible. She was leaning over the actor who was playing Dorian Gray so she could touch up his make-up, a palette of foundation in her hand. A palette that, musically, would have been a cascade of bells, the sound only slightly more high-pitched than her laughter.

I stopped at the last row of seats in the room and waited for her to straighten up. She was wearing a short skirt, black. A midnight-blue T-shirt hugged the curve of her back. No bra. Leather sandals with a worn strap. A mass of red hair, precariously held back by a hairdresser's clip that seemed exhausted by the effort of taming the strands that were waiting to escape its scrutiny and fly off in all directions.

I saw all of this, and a lot more. The lines that her arms traced, the stroke of her wrist as she moved a little brush across the actor's cheeks; he, eyes closed, surrendered to her. I saw the crease of her knee and a vein, so blue it was green, snaking up the length of her leg before disappearing under the hem of her skirt.

I saw a mark left behind by a mosquito beneath her right elbow and smudges of freckles all over her skin.

I saw…

The theatre was a little grimy and gave off the smell of dust and sweat. The upholstered seats had seen better days. The lighting was concentrated on the stage, where designers bustled about, along with two or three other guys whose roles in this strange ballet, now in its first rehearsal, I was unsure of.

I saw the garnet-red velour divan that the actor was stretched across. A lamp with a fringed shade, its light too bright. A portrait turned to face the wall.

The voices of two or three others reached me, although I didn't understand what they were talking about. Their intonation was different to what I was used to in the small Parisian venues where I had first performed.

In the duration of a minim, I had forgotten that I was in London, that this was my first truly serious job. For me, life had begun in that exact place, at that very moment.

Everything came back to me when the girl stood up

straight and left the stage, not to return. I still didn't know who she was. However, I did know that I was no longer the same person.

I would never have imagined those bells could come from a girl. I'd always been particularly fond of the sound of the triangle. It reminded me of perfectly formed raindrops falling into a swollen river. A perfect bluish transparency; a magnifying mirror. Everything travelling at such speed that the imaginary took precedence over reality.

But *voilà*. That day, in London, I met Our Lady of the Bells. And she came into my life at such a speed that I am still trying to catch her.

Liv – that was her name – was a make-up artist for the stage. She loved pistachio ice cream, scones only when warm and stuffed with raisins, the rain when it was regular, the sun at dusk, the grey of cobblestones, literature – but nothing penned after 1937 – French vineyards, Barcelona, and the British Royal Family.

All of this I discovered little by little, as I added touches of colour to the portrait of her that took root in me over time. With Liv, image and reality often overlapped, only to then become so far apart that I no longer recognised the woman that slept at my side.

But that July day in London, it had not yet come to that.

I had landed in the city two nights earlier. I had been hired to compose the music for a new adaptation of *The Picture of Dorian Gray*. One of my favourite novels. One of my cult authors. A city I loved. That was all it took for me to jump at the chance, accepting all the conditions: pitiful pay, miserable accommodation, a ridiculously tiny budget. I was twenty-five years old and took myself seriously, but not so seriously that I would let such an opportunity pass me by. I had imagined myself as bilingual, thanks to proper schooling and my own painstaking efforts to learn English. I soon became disabused of this notion, but the new notes that this language promised me more than made up for the initial difficulty I had when conversing. These notes made their way through me, giving rise to new perspectives, to new associations that it took me a while to accept as my own.

I had spent the first two days of my stay taking myself on walks whichever way the wind blew, from Soho to St James's Park, from Covent Garden to the banks of the Thames. London was noisy, lively, crazy. I passed men in sad, severe suits, girls with mauve hair pulled up into nests on top of their heads, old, dignified, upright ladies on their way back from Harrods, trendy couples diving into the narrow streets of Soho. On the double-decker bus, one had the feeling of living each and every bend under threat of the next branch of a London plane. The tourists let little cries slip out, the children applauded.

I delighted in all the sounds, all the colours, the hues of summer on the yellowed lawns. I was beside myself, and I couldn't care less that the shower water was lukewarm at best, that my flatmates had a decided taste for Blur, preferably very late at night and played very loudly, that my bedroom was the size of a little bathroom in a provincial hotel in France. I was ready to gorge on Indian food, on stew, on fish and chips, on sushi, on everything offered to me by this worldly city where a cacophony of sounds, scents and colours reigned. These synthesisations were incredible. From Chelsea to Brixton, Seven Sisters to Greenwich, from Notting Hill to Piccadilly, the whole planet was there before my eyes – the dazzled eyes of a Frenchman, somewhat conformist, a little strait-laced, for whom wearing velvet trousers and a scarf around his neck felt like the height of rebellion. As for contemporary music, I had stopped at the Beatles, at Christophe, at the Stones, and I had looked no further.

Two days of uninterrupted strolls had birthed a symphony within me that I was sure would enchant the play's director – thrill him.

It must be said, however, that my encounter with Liv aside, the new adaptation of Wilde's classic failed to live up to its promise.

'Téo, get a move on, you're going to be late!'

A grunt, heavy footsteps on the stairs and Téo appears in the kitchen, unkempt, hunched over as if he were carrying the weight of the world on his shoulders, sporting a T-shirt from the day before, and the day before that.

I open my mouth, then close it again. It's not worth commenting on. The kid couldn't care less.

This T-shirt, made in Bangladesh, 100% cotton, machine wash at 40°C recommended, has been worn for three consecutive days and nights. According to the World Health Organisation, it would be suitable to…

I hold back a smile that is inevitably erased when Téo strikes out at Laïvely, shutting her up. Bab, half in earnest, half in jest, pipes up, 'Since when did that thing have eyes?'

It's true. Since when has Laïvely been able to see us? In fact, can she see us? Or is she simply able to smell the odour that is emanating from Téo as he settles down in front of his cereal and mug of fair-trade coffee? Because, yes, he stinks. As soon as he lifts his mug to carry it to his lips, all the while stooping his neck to avoid too big a movement that would be detrimental to his hunched back, a sweet-and-sour aroma wafts towards my nose. But there's no reason Laïvely should have a sense of smell. That's not what I was aiming for when I created her.

I scrunch up my nose and avoid responding to Bab, who has already moved on to something else. She's preparing her lunch box to take to the swimming pool with her. A few months ago, when she and Téo had just moved in, she would come back to have lunch with me. She had the time. Then, little by little, she started to take up this new habit, always with a good excuse: a break cut short due to a colleague being off sick, a private lesson that had been added to her schedule, the need to run an errand. Without me ever really realising, our lunches for two have become an exception. Now, she doesn't return to the house until her day has come to an end. And for my part, I don't offer to meet her for a picnic at Buttes-Chaumont, or at a brasserie in the neighbourhood so we can spend a romantic couple of hours together. I have neither the desire nor the courage.

Lisa has already left for school. I finish my coffee pensively. Two little notes have been obsessing me for days, yet I still haven't been able to extract a melody from them. Maybe I would if I went for a walk? No, I'll be better off in my studio, with my instruments. What's more, the weather is unpredictable. There's a risk of rain. I don't feel like getting soaked.

Téo finishes and leaves everything spread across the table, his place adorned with varying and diverse stains. Before I can venture even the smallest criticism, his mother has already piled the dirty dishes in the sink, wiped a sponge across the table and put the milk back in the fridge.

I sigh. Is she just on autopilot, or is it a tactic to avoid yet another argument about the kids? Laïvely flickers softly. It's like she's winking. Having made sure that Bab's back is truly turned, I wink back at her. On top of everything else, there's no need to provoke a fit of jealously that a tube stuffed with electronics doesn't merit being the object of.

'See you this evening, Stan. Have a good day.' Bab leans over, gives me a light peck on the lips and leaves without looking back.

The door closes behind her and Téo, who still hasn't uttered a single word.

Laïvely lights up. It's like a smile on the face of a loved one.

It's my turn to leave the kitchen, happy, yet uneasy at the same time.

London

'Do you want to go for a drink?'

It had been ten days since I saw Liv for the first time. In the meantime, I had officially introduced myself and discovered her open, animated face, her green eyes, her smooth skin, the dimple on her right cheek and the beauty spot next to her right eye. Her smile had become familiar, as had the tone of her voice and her adorable accent whenever she tried to speak to me in French, her voice dropping an octave, her lips stumbling over each U, unpronounceable on that side of the channel.

I had eaten lunch with her and some members of the company several times, all of whom agreed that Max, the director, was a talentless arsehole. They also agreed that the idea that Dorian, in turning round the portrait, discovers himself in the guise of a woman was as ridiculous as it was … sexist? ill-timed? out of place? Max Canut may well have claimed that it was, on the contrary, a powerful symbol, but we all feared that audiences and critics alike would miss the point completely. For Max, Dorian (and therefore Oscar Wilde) was deeply terrified of his femininity, of his homosexuality (the former, latent and nothing but the fruit of Max's imagination, and the latter, completely assumed). I wasn't a psychologist, but I couldn't help wondering if it wasn't his own sexual preferences that Max was questioning, although, since Wilde, Britain had made a lot of progress on that front. The director therefore thought it normal that when Dorian confronted his portrait, it should reflect back to him a vision of the feminine in a crudely transvestite guise. Max could easily talk to us for hours about Dorian in drag – he thought his idea was ground-breaking, fantastic, marvellous. But what could have been more fantastic than having the face of the man who subscribed to all those vile acts hold on to all the charm and beauty of youth, whilst the painting, that terrible portrait of him, displayed day after day the marks of his disavowals, his vices, his crimes?

We were therefore rather dubious – myself more than anyone else, because, at the moment that was supposed to mark the climax of the story, Max wanted my music to be a mixture of punk, Gregorian chants and Red Army hymns. I couldn't imagine what he was hoping to hear by mixing all of that together. He, on the other hand, had a very clear idea of the sound it would create. Unfortunately, I had so far proven myself incapable of providing him with what he was so impatiently waiting for.

One lunchtime, as we all sat outside on a lawn yellowed by the heat to eat our meals bought from the nearest McDonald's, Laila, who worked in wardrobe – early forties, self-assured, blunt, always spoke her mind – tried to reassure me.

'Don't you worry. Max is always like this. It's not the first time I've worked with him. Last time, at quite a niche festival in Cornwall, he put on an adaption of Shakespeare's life transplanted into an Orwellian universe. It was super weird and confused, and the music – my god.' She frantically waved a hand armed with a greasy fry loaded with ketchup, which flew onto her T-shirt, staining it like drops of blood.

I was unsuccessful in getting anything more out of her on the subject. Eventually, Max heard the music, but he never found anyone to transcribe it, ever.

Laila also ended up admitting that I was the third person Max had called for this job. That didn't reassure me about my future in London as a young, French composer prodigy.

And that pushed me to invite Liv to go out for a drink.

'Do you want to go for a drink?'

It was normal to invite a girl out for a drink when one was twenty-five years old. And yet...

Of course, I was already acquainted with the female body. In Paris, in bars, on nights out, young women seemed to find an unrealistic charm in my artistic side (cursed, thus penniless) and they rarely refused me. We would chat for a while, my old, velvet corduroy trousers suddenly seeming to them the height of fashion and romanticism. They would even show surprise at my sobriety (a cursed, penniless artist must surely be a drunk or an addict) before they came to the conclusion that I must be suffering from an ulcer or cirrhosis of some sort, and that even one drink would kill me. Abstinence couldn't be a deliberate choice, because who would deprive themselves of anything at that age? Reassured by the image they had created of me, they allowed me between their sheets, between their thighs.

But often, the sun had not yet risen before I left. I found the intimacy that came in the aftermath of making love insufferable. I couldn't stand the kind of coffee that was drunk together the morning after, the unformulated question of whether this night would be followed by another. I only had the desire to go back home, take a long, hot shower, shave and get to work.

Those interludes had a negative effect on me that I have never been able to explain. Far from inspiring me, they actually cut me off from any capacity to create. I would spend the day in front of my piano, growing more and more depressed hour after hour, only capable of interpreting old jazz standards or Debussy (why him and no one else? the mystery remains), as if emptied of all substance.

After several experiences of that ilk, it quickly became clear that I needed to reduce my frolicking with girls I met in bars or jazz clubs in Saint-Germain-des-Prés and Halles to a minimum. And it was also vital to recognise that it seemed I was incapable of falling in love. The act of sex killed all the music within me, although I was convinced that love, on the other hand, would increase my talent tenfold. We're like that when we're young. Full of certainties, rational explanations for things that are absolutely not so, on a quest for answers that we believe to be original yet are nothing more than stereotypes.

I was no different.

But Liv, she was something else.

To start with, she had never, at any moment, appeared to be attracted to or seduced by the things that made me (relatively) successful in London: my French accent, my laid-back approach, the silk scarf around my neck. On the contrary. When we were introduced to each other, she had quickly evaluated me, her eyes moving from my rebellious lock of hair to my suede shoes before passing once more over my face. A little smile (that I had interpreted as mocking) was sketched across the corners of her lips. She held out her slim hand to me, graceful and soft, and murmured an '*enchantée*' of the most formal kind, before turning on her heels and heading towards the wings.

I didn't know until later, much later, that in that moment she'd realised, at first sight, that I had the power to bring her a happiness she had never experienced before, but also to make her suffer – the other side of the eternal coin that comes with love. She had refused to experience both sides, the price of being happy too high for what she carried in her emotional baggage. At twenty-two years old she had already had her heart broken once, starting again was out of the question. Never. She preferred to let her turn pass her by, ignore the most beautiful love in the world, content as a single woman with her salt-and-vinegar crisps on a Friday night. Perhaps, one day in the distant future, she would live with a suitable man who she didn't hate, and that would be good enough. Gone were any lyrical flights of fancy, declarations of love whispered in the early hours of the morning on the banks of the Thames, weekends in Brighton, holidays to the Highlands, scones at teatime in St Andrews. Gone were the promises of 'always' and 'forever'. She wouldn't fall into that trap again, she'd already given enough, thank you very much.

'Do you want to go for a drink?'

'Yeah, OK,' she responded with a smile.

And my heart dropped into my stomach. Her 'yeah' contained the purity of a nightingale's song, the grace of the gentle summer tide in La Baule, the lightness of the wind in the Corsican pines. It was powder pink, with a touch of raspberry red at its heart. It had the aroma of orange blossom.

I blushed, stammered, asked her to meet me outside the theatre that evening, and ran off.

Shut in my studio in the Rabbit Hole, I hum the two notes that will not leave me. But, perhaps for the first time in my life, I cannot seem to associate a single colour with them. Something that is more than unsettling.

I have always lived with these odd associations. Tastes, sounds and colours all form an amalgam within me that only music can regulate. Music is the one thing that allows them to come together, to join each other, to associate, but also to detach from each other just enough to give each element a coherence that would otherwise be lacking from the ensemble.

For a long time, I had believed that there was nothing particularly special about this phenomenon, that everyone had the same experience. When my mother introduced me to *La Traviata*, which to this day remains my favourite opera, I could make out pastel rainbows, violet and orange storms, the taste of fresh strawberries and cauliflower *au gratin*, all dependent on the act, the scene, the aria. She laughed when, as the music had flowed, I revealed what she called my 'visions'. It quickly became a game that the whole family would play on Sundays when my grandparents came to visit.

I grew up in Limousin on a farm that to my young eyes was vast, the green of the pastures and the more sombre shapes of the groves dotted with cows and dogs. I was the third of five. We were free, for the most part, to occupy ourselves however we pleased, and we didn't go without.

School was part of our day-to-day life, as were the fights that were typical among siblings. The radio was always tuned into RMC, spitting it out all day long as it trembled to the rhythm of my father's footsteps – he never strayed too far from it. The kitchen smelt like tarte tatin, rhubarb, wet dog or veal stew, depending on the day or the season. The world, for me, ended at the borders of the region, but the departure of my brother, six years older than me, marked the death of that belief. Admittedly, I had already embarked on several trips to Paris, Poitiers and Limoges, but these hadn't altered my faith in the permanence of the farm, in the absurd conviction that everything else was nothing but a fragile embellishment susceptible to change at any moment. Life took it upon itself to prove to me that while I wasn't completely wrong, my basic assumption was false. It was, in fact, the farm of my childhood that could be scratched from reality as if it had never existed; the cities, on the other hand, made a fool of the passing of time.

Vincent then, after finishing school, left for Bordeaux to study law.

My sister, Yvonne, who sorrowfully bore our paternal grandmother's name, followed.

My turn would come. I was not in a rush.

I would listen to the tune of the water in the stream. I could spend hours fascinated by the sound of raindrops falling onto the leaves of the apple tree in front of the barn. I focused on Dagobert's breath – a deaf and blind Great Dane that I had always known as part of the household. With age, he had developed a form of asthma, and his tumultuous, broken breathing recalled the creamy chestnut hues of vanilla ice cream flavoured with rum.

I was a studious pupil with decent results, though lacking brilliance, as I was too easily distracted by a sound, a glimmer or the creak of a chair. I drew strange shapes in the margins of my workbooks and spent more time colouring them in than doing my exercises, which would slowly disappear beneath the green, the red and the yellow of my pencils.

An old, untuned piano lay abandoned in our living room, its innards nibbled by greedy mice. It was on this piano that I played my first chords. And thanks to this piano, years later I found myself in London and in Liv's arms.

I close my eyes, the two notes resonate through me. Time draws out, withers, spreads like a thin crêpe batter on Candlemas. The taste reaches my mouth, the scent rises to my nostrils.

Crêpe batter recipe, Laïvely suddenly sings out.

Startled, I'm pulled out of my daydream. She reels off the list of ingredients, suggests accompaniments. I listen attentively.

I must have spoken out loud for her to react like this. I hadn't realised, but it does sometimes happen to me. Only last week I was caught out in the supermarket. I was sure I had kept to myself the all-important question of where to find the sanitary towels that Babette had added to the list at the last minute, when a young woman with an amused smirk on her lips pointed me towards the right aisle, which I proceeded to rush towards, bright red and mumbling an inaudible thank-you.

Laïvely shuts up, plunges into a silence filled with expectation. I know this, not because I attribute human characteristics to her (only her voice is human) but because her green light is flashing softly.

'Thank you.'

She lets out a soft sigh. *You're welcome.*

The green light goes out. I shiver.

I don't feel like crêpes anymore. Or anything, for that matter.

Maybe Babette is right. The Rabbit Hole is going to end up swallowing me.

Evening has arrived. I haven't left the house all day and now it's too late.

Laïvely, who I finally placed on the sideboard in the hallway in an attempt to persuade myself that without her in the room I would be able to concentrate, joyfully greets Lisa when she returns. As for me, I don't move from my piano stool, to which I have been anchored for hours. My studio is plunged in darkness, the shadows having slowly gnawed at the colours and the white of the walls.

Lisa, on her way to her bedroom upstairs, stops in front of my door without knocking. She learned from an early age not to disturb me. A closed door means that I do not want company, that I am composing. I'm not going to bother to set her straight on the subject. She should be allowed to hold on to the weak belief that an unalterable norm still exists, resistant to all the upheavals in our lives. If only she knew, poor girl, that for months now I haven't put a single note down on paper ... I hear her sigh, I even seem to feel the gentle rush of air as she goes to push down the handle, and then nothing. A second later I hear her light footsteps, almost spectral, on the stairs, then the creak of another door, her bedroom. Silence returns, even more opaque, even more suffocating.

Téo and Babette return a little later, together. Laïvely's tone is drier when she greets them, wishing them a good evening. The image of hazelnuts crosses my mind. For Lisa, it was something more like well-ripened apricots, juicy.

In the kitchen Babette busies herself with preparing dinner. It's as if the day has not taken place, as if all the hours have been wiped away with a damp cloth. She is standing before the sink with her back to me, in the same position she adopted this morning at breakfast. Téo, no chattier, is sitting at the table crunching on crisps. Lisa is most likely still shut in her bedroom.

I kiss Babette on the neck. My lips feel cold, far too cold for a tender kiss. In fact, she shivers, and I notice that goosebumps stand to attention on her neck. The expression 'kiss of death' comes to mind. But no such thing exists.

Death strikes you, but it doesn't put its mouth to yours

for one last, tender embrace. Only at the pen of J.K. Rowling do dementors suck out your soul and feed on it, their kiss signalling your end. In life, death is far less subtle, far less elegant than that; it beats you up, cracks you, breaks your bones, suffocates you by shoving its great force down on your face. It's always vulgar.

'Hey, have you had a good day?'

What better than the banal to bring one's feet back down to earth? I have no desire to spend yet another evening cut off from others, like the prisoner of an invisible plastic film that prevents me from understanding them, from touching them, that gives me the sensation that their words are distorted, always off the mark. I have to return to the land of the living. I've done it before, haven't I? At least I think I have.

'Yeah, good. You?' Bab replies without even turning around.

I have never known anyone wash carrots with so much zeal. It's a fascinating spectacle. And it seems to last for hours, like a long tracking shot in slow motion. The water trickles over the dry skin on her hands. She has short fingers, a little masculine. Her nails are trimmed short, clean. She holds the carrots two by two. No matter their length. She moves them back and forth under the stream of water in an immutable two-beat rhythm. I could almost beat it out, easily turn it into a little song. Water droplets splash onto the work surface, onto Babette's T-shirt. She couldn't care less. She places the two carrots down, grabs two more and starts again. Only then, leaning over the bin, does she play the peeler. Her movements are alert, lively, assured. She only passes over the same spot once, never twice. The results are perfect, always.

Then she places them on a plate, removes the apparatus that enables them to be grated from the cupboard, turns it to the finest setting, cuts the veg-etables into three equal parts, puts them into the machine, and turns it on. The sound is deafening for two minutes fifty-two seconds. I've already timed it.

The countdown is on if I want to get out of there before the noise. I stroke her arm before slipping away as I mumble, 'I'll go and see what Lisa's up to.'

Fully immersed in her task, Babette doesn't hear me.

I climb the stairs in silence, the softness of the wood of the handrail sinking into the palm of my hand. It has been smoothed by the passage of time, skated by all the fingers that have ceaselessly caressed it. Like everything else in the Rabbit Hole, it tells a story, but it's shrewd, capable of keeping its secrets. I arrive at the landing on the second floor just as the rumble of the grater reverberates through the walls of the house, rolling through it in a devastating wave, ready to destroy everything in its path.

Lisa's room is the first on the right. Not a single noise escapes from it; there's not even a hint of light coming from beneath her door. I hesitate. My daughter likes silence, darkness. Sometimes, I'm afraid she will discreetly fade away, little by little, and I won't notice until it is too late.

I'm about to knock, I hold my breath.

My arm falls to the side of my body.

I persuade myself that it's better to leave her alone, calm, when in reality it is simply that I don't know how to talk to her anymore.

I go back down a floor. From my bedroom at the end of the corridor, I hear a murmur. I prick up my ears, move furtively towards it. The music becomes clearer.

Doris Day.

Que sera, sera.

What will be, will be…

Liv's favourite song.

I close my eyes. The sound rises. The memories drown me. I let myself slide down the wall of the hallway, tears in my eyes. Perfectly formed tears that would produce the tinkling sound of bells should they fall onto water.

London

TWENTY YEARS EARLIER

Then came that first drink, of which I hold only vague and confused memories. A pub, laughter, noise, shouting, beer. And Our Lady of the Bells in front of me. The first night was clumsy, pleasureless, made up of timid gestures and curbed desire of the kind that only occurs in great love stories. Afterwards, I lay stretched out on my back, short of breath, a taste of papaya on my tongue. Liv pretended to sleep at my side, curled up, her back to me. Her even breathing couldn't fool me, my ear had always been able to discern the tiniest variations of breath, which I owe as much to my numerous siblings as to poor Dagobert and his asthma.

There was a coffee the day after that sleepless night, shared with blushing cheeks and a strange sparkle in our glances. As if Liv also knew. As if she knew that there would be a before and an after, but that there was still time, for a few minutes only, to believe that nothing had changed.

We left together for another rehearsal at the

theatre, keeping a few dozen centimetres between us on the crowded pavement, taking care not to brush against one another. And then, once we had arrived, she hurried off to the dressing rooms with a quick goodbye, her fingertips hanging in the air, and I joined my piano.

I played it like I had never played it before after a night of sex. I let it carry me away, tapping the keys, first briskly, with energy, then gently, caressing them, pleading them, charming them. They resisted for a moment before submitting themselves, meeting me and granting me what I asked of them.

I don't know how long this lasted. But when I finally lifted my head, my eyes brimming with purple carnations, the silence on the stage was heavy, technicians and actors frozen like victims of a spell.

The first to shake off the torpor was the director. Max snorted, 'Come on, Stan. That is NOT it. Really, not at all. Dorian CANNOT fall in love with the feminine representation of himself. You've completely twisted my idea!' He stormed out of the room, stamping his feet and grumbling, cursing so-called musicians, who did they think they were, incapable of understanding the most detailed information, imagining themselves as the next Mozart when not even someone taking the tube would waste a second listening to the mindless cacophony they insisted on producing.

My eyes found Liv's. She smiled. She was a fresh fruit salad in spring, scattered with fine shavings of mint.

We were in love.

The next day, unsurprisingly, Max gave me my notice.

I moved into Liv's small bedroom. She shared a narrow, crooked house with two other young girls whose names I have never remembered, and who, like Liv, worked in theatre.

I spent the first days of our cohabitation with my eyes glued to the ceiling, glimpsing strange shapes and colours, letting the music of our love take hold of me. There, I waited for her like a faithful dog, and only came to life when she returned.

Then we would go out for a walk in the city burdened with heat and pollution. Now we strolled hand in hand, talking, kissing, falling into silences as we were taken along according to our moods, always in harmony.

After a while I ended up doing a tour of the pubs, offering to play in the evenings. I had become an entertainer, my wages collected in a hat passed round the room, no longer worried about what tomorrow would bring. I lived from one day to the next, something that kept me busy full-time, something that required my absolute attention. As a result, not a second of those moments has managed to escape me, run from me. I still savour each one with the same delight.

I was learning about Liv's body, both in love and in the most mundane, everyday gestures. Her hand as she lifted it to her hair to reposition a rebel strand (of which there were several) drew a perfect arch, a half-circle that resembled a moon as luminous as the sun. Her belly quivered beneath a precise caress. The scar on her ankle from a stubborn bicycle pedal.

I was learning about her background, her family, the flavours of Sunday roast potatoes, Christmas dinners after the queen's speech and copious amounts of Buck's Fizz. I discovered the colour of her school uniform and the tie that she took care to loosen, carelessly, as soon as she crossed the threshold of the school doors. I could smell the perfumes of the powdered make-up and the nail varnishes that her and her little sister spent hours playing with as children. I saw the landscapes of her summer holidays, Emma Peel's smile and the shadow of John Steed's hat cast over his face. Everything was exotic to my senses; everything was a source of wonder.

Then summer finally gave way to autumn, to the fog, to the insidiously piercing rain. Our walks became impromptu afternoon teas on her bed to escape the babbling of her flatmates. Max's play sunk like a lead balloon before the press release had even been sent out. Liv looked for work in the West End whilst offering her services in hospitals to women left distraught, pale and browless by cancer.

It was there she met Ellie Zienstein. And our life took a new direction.

'What shall we do this weekend?' Babette asks as she stretches out lazily by my side.

Her skin is soft, pink. My fingers piano across her hip, searching for the desire of the early days. I roll on top of her, wrap my thighs around her, grab her wrists. She laughs, arches her back, and offers herself. I enter her.

Playing at Music City today, at two-thirty pm, is… starts Laïvely, in an undoubtedly grumpy tone.

Babette doesn't seem to realise; when making love she has the capacity to completely close herself off from whatever is not the vibrations of her body; she becomes preoccupied with seeking out pleasure. Her breath becomes short and her eyes close. Sometimes I wonder what dreams she is finding refuge in so as to reach orgasm.

I accelerate the rhythm, wanting to satisfy her, and gently caress her left breast with my tongue.

A moan escapes her, covering up Laïvely's loquaciousness – she's speaking faster and faster, as if to drown out the colourful sounds rising from Babette's throat.

I close my eyes in turn, letting myself get carried away by the music that these two rivals are creating. It's *Aida*, it's violent, it's Jean-Michel Jarre facing a human sea, it's Marilyn Monroe's hoarse voice when she's in love, it's...

Babette lets out one last cry. It's my turn to finish.

She holds me tightly against her, I see the yellow of a fluffy chick and fluorescent green, bordered by black and charcoal grey. Then it all blends together, and all that remains is the colour of the North Sea on a rainy day, a hue between that of a wet pavement and a sheet that was once white but has turned grey with each wash.

'Oh, Stan...'

Laïvely is silent. But she's listening to us. I know she is.

She's great, Babette. If Liv was a complex symphony – a complexity heightened by the fact that we didn't share the same mother tongue and had to be more attentive to everything that a facial expression or the movement of a body part said – Babette is a light jingle from the 1960s. She laughs out loud, a deep laugh that completely occupies the space that surrounds her. She likes her curves, her fullness, her unmanageable hair that curls, then becomes frizzy.

She likes her swimming-instructor flip-flops, the moisture in the air of the pool, almost tropical, and the dry slap of wind when she leaves the suffocating atmosphere. She likes strawberry jam and cream-of-chestnut tarts, which she bakes to perfection. Dry cakes leave her lost for words, as do teas with shadowy flavours. She prefers deep infusions – elderflower, orange, anything that reminds her of sugar. She knows nothing about music, beside Britney Spears (in the years before she fizzled out) and for her, 'Toxic' is the quintessence of musical perfection. She can put the song on loop or watch the video clip ten times in a row, still fascinated by the way the light plays with the singer's costume – an outfit that leaves nothing to the imagination. She only reads bestsellers once they've been published in paperback. She prefers Mary Higgins Clark to Camilla Läckberg, Virginie Grimaldi to Aurélie Valognes, Lévy's page turners to Musso's, she loves *Fifty Shades of Grey* (the films too), and shows open contempt for classics from earlier centuries, with a particular aversion to Shakespeare, who earned her an F in her French oral exam.

She is simple, Babette, on the surface. She doesn't speak about the past, even less so about Téo's father, who disappeared shortly after the boy's birth, never to return. She has fought her whole life, Babette, but she can't stand the dumbed-down discourse surrounding single women's lives, the difficulties they face, the harshness of their existence. She laughs, shrugs it off, until her face lights up with the memory of something cheeky her little baby once did.

She is positive, Babette. She doesn't wallow in sadness and darkness. She prefers the light of summer days, sunflowers and daffodils.

It's all of this that drew me to her. Her ability to live in the moment, to avoid the false comfort of a nostalgia that devastates the soul and the present. Her smile and the sparkle in her midnight-blue eyes when she uses irony rather than tears to get herself out of a delicate situation.

In some ways, she has subtly managed, I don't know how, to instil in me enough desire to live that she has made me human again.

Things may be complicated now, but I've not forgotten the many things that brought us closer and bound us together, beyond our day-to-day life in the Rabbit Hole. And occasionally, when things are becoming too sombre, I think back to our smiles on that summer day she took me out on a bike ride to Versailles. We'd pedalled through the park on our bikes before flopping down in the shade of an immense tree, a weeping willow that had surely welcomed others into its arms. We had a picnic there before dozing off, leaning on one another, innocently, in the drowsiness of summer. It was a badly behaved pug that woke us up. It alternated between drooling and licking, to the horrified cries of the owner, a Versailles girl, born and bred, who seemed to think the park belonged to her. We finished the day by savouring a horribly expensive and just as chemical ice cream. We'd laughed on the train that took us back to Paris, at the red stains on Babette's tongue left by the strawberry flavour, and the green on mine, perfumed with mint.

Babette and I met at the swimming pool, of course. It was a November evening. I was the last in the pool. I tallied my lengths to drown out the noise in my head. I concentrated on nothing but the music that my hands composed as they penetrated the water of the pool with each movement of my arms; I was submerged in an immutable rhythm. Her strident blow of the whistle dragged me out of this hypnotic torpor that I had let drag me along. She laughed when I stopped at her feet, stunned.

'Sir, we're closing…'

Her voice reminded me of the marshmallows of my childhood that I ate at fairgrounds and festivals. It had their somewhat chewy consistency, their taste.

And it was the first time in a long time that colours, as pale as they were, had come to me at the sound of a voice.

I came across her again by chance, outside the entrance to the pool – we were the last ones to leave. She walked towards the metro, and I accompanied her, simply to take advantage of a few more moments in which to remember the sweetness of those marshmallows.

Now, we live together. Or we try, in any case. And if it's failing, I'm the only one to blame.

When I woke up that Sunday, I decided I wouldn't go into my studio once in the whole day. It's eleven o'clock, and so far, I've kept my promise to myself. Babette has been asking me for weeks to do something about the door down to the garage, which squeaks horribly and sticks halfway. I get stuck into it as she helps Téo with his homework. Given that he has no interest in school (or anything else for that matter), I prefer to stay away from his room at moments like this. I don't know how Lisa can stand the sharp shards of loud voices that escape from there. There's nothing sweet or sugary about Babette's voice in those moments. It's more like a bitter orange sprinkled with ground cayenne pepper. I shudder. As for Téo's, it's symbols crashing out of time with the rest of the orchestra. Insufferable.

I've brought Laïvely with me. She's playing *Après la pluie* by Satie. As always, the choice is judicious. The perfection of the piano notes, the simplicity of the composition, make it, to my ears, a piece with a beauty that is difficult to equal.

The garage serves as a storage room. There are still boxes in here that I brought over from London with me and remain unopened. When we returned, I didn't have the courage to unpack anything but the essentials. And later, I found that there was nothing in the boxes that I missed enough to justify sorting them out.

I notice the ominous '*miscellaneous*' is written on some of them. I know they contain a whole jumble of unimportant papers, old recipes, stones picked up on one hike or another through the Scottish lochs, old chestnut leaves that have turned into dust, love notes that were once stuck to a bathroom mirror, electric cables with plugs that are useless for French sockets. I would certainly find a lock of Lisa's baby hair, her first scribbles, which Liv framed with the same respect one would frame Turner's watercolours, an old slipper knitted by her grandmother, and who knows what else.

I'm not ready to get rid of it, nor to rummage through the memories.

So I leave the pile, turn away with a shrug of the shoulders, and look for my tools, which are probably somewhere on my right. I'm going to attempt to repair that uncooperative door.

I don't dare tell Babette, but the door's always been this way. The first time I set foot in the Rabbit Hole it was already squeaking.

My great-aunt had just bought the house. Its façade was not yet adorned with illustrations pulled from the pages of *Alice in Wonderland*. She would have them painted a few years later, as Elisabeth, her only child, was crazy about the fairy tale. Personally, I never liked the story. The hysterical rabbit terrified me, the king and the queen distressed me, and as for Alice herself, I found her disturbing. Over the years, I've been told over and over to re-read this classic, particularly in its original language, but I've never found the time nor the urge.

My first stay here then, left me with few memories, as there was nothing original about the house that captured my childlike attention, aside from the niggling squeaking sound of the garage door. I amused myself with it for hours, opening and closing it for much of the afternoon, to the great displeasure of my mother and her cousin. I'm not sure why we'd gone to visit Paris that day. It was probably for one of my medical appointments, which form nothing more than a blurry cluster in my memory.

In any case, when the second stay at Aunt Agathe's came around, Alice and the rabbit ran amok across the façade. Today, their colours have faded a little, but they still carry the fate of that place firmly in their not-so-innocent hands.

Elisabeth died as a teenager the year I started school. I think our parents hid the tragedy from us for a long time out of fear that it would traumatise us. I didn't think of the house again for many years, it had slipped from my mind, just like Aunt Agathe, who I had only met a handful of times. It was in London that I learned of her death, and that she had left me the house. I don't know with what sleight of hand she had made me the heir. My sister and brothers didn't hold it against me; they had other fish to fry at the time. The eldest was in the middle of a divorce. The next two were either building their lives or unravelling them, as we all tend to do in our thirties. The youngest was still living at home – she'd decided that she would take on the farm one day.

Me, I was happy, I was composing and living with Liv, and that alone was more than enough to fill the cracks in my life. I took a quick trip to Paris to sign the papers and didn't busy myself with anything else. I didn't even bother to put the house on the market. Once I'd signed all of the paperwork I took the opportunity to pass by the place, checked the water was off, played with the garage door for a few minutes, went up to the first floor, then carried on up the stairs to the second floor, walking past rooms that I didn't recognise, rooms in which I had probably never set foot before. The whole place smelt of dust and sadness, cloaked in a heavy atmosphere of mourning and loss. My aunt's furniture was old and imposing, eating up light and space. The only thing I took was a collection of Baudelaire's poetry, in an edition that was pleasing to the eye and pleasant to the touch, and an old pink rococo barrette, which I thought Liv would like.

And so, life went on.

It was not until after the tragedy, long after, that I remembered the house. My older brother Vincent wanted me to come back to France, where it would be easier to look after me (his words, not mine). The others supported him. Why stay in London? We'd lived there self-sufficiently, Liv and I, withdrawn into our love, which occupied all of our time, which nourished our creative energy. There was Lisa, of course; Lisa, whose name was formed of letters that belonged to us. Our sun, our star, our unbreakable, inseparable link.

I ended up giving in. After all, it was all the same there, or anywhere...

Vincent sorted everything out: he installed mains electrics, checked the boiler, fitted a more modern and functional kitchen. He piled all of Aunt Agathe's things into a bedroom on the second floor – things he thought I'd like to keep. The rest of the house was just waiting for our furniture and the scattered remnants of our lives.

It was raining on the day we arrived with the movers. It was cold, even though Vincent had taken the precaution of turning the heating on the day before. I shivered as I gave confused instructions to the bruisers who were staggering under the weight of our life. Lisa had taken refuge in the room on the second floor where Vincent had stuffed the furniture Agathe had left behind. She was rummaging through the bazaar of objects, diving into a past that was not ours, forgetting for a while the mass of sorrow that made up our memories.

At first, we lived holed up on the ground floor. Our bedrooms upstairs waited for us. The movers had put our beds, furniture, boxes of books and clothes up there. Lisa hadn't wanted to keep any toys from 'ours'.

Of her mother's she had kept the famous barrette, brought from the Rabbit Hole, and a hairbrush. On her bed, she would only accept the patchwork quilt that Liv had had since childhood. As for me, I'd conserved her last small bottle of perfume, her make-up bag and a ridiculous wig that she had bought for a fancy-dress party years before. Her teddy bear too. A sort of Paddington knock-off, his fur a little thin in places, thanks to the passing of time and the many cuddles he had received. Liv told me she had still slept with him up until we met. He knew everything about her: her lovers, her sadnesses, her friendships. He had been her closest and most faithful confidant.

The bedrooms then, remained uninhabited whilst we huddled on the large sofa in the living room. We rarely opened the shutters. I continued to drink a lot, and Lisa clung on to silence. Liv's absence was not at all easier on this side of the Channel.

It was not Vincent – he's far too rational for that – but Julie, my youngest sister, who eventually dragged us out of our lethargy. She had given up on the farm years before, after the divorce of our parents. She'd stayed there a while to watch our father sink into despair and alcoholism. Wounds like that, she knew how to care for them. She tackled ours.

She won us over, little by little. She gently interfered in our day-to-day lives. She made us, without ever raising her voice or using coercion, wash. She made us eat too – something other than crisps and badly defrosted pizzas.

She slowly reintroduced music to the house in little touches. First humming, then singing. Songs from our childhood, French folklore, then songs from the forties, fifties and sixties. Then the 1970s arrived, and I joined her in the choruses, my voice quiet, hushed. When we moved on to the 1980s, I was able to enter my bedroom, and Lisa hers. With the songs of the following decade, I scaled another floor to set up my studio next to the bedroom of relics, as we had nick-named the room in which the remains of my aunt's life were squeezed.

We did not go any further, it wasn't necessary. Then, I started to play the piano again, like the victim of an accident who was rediscovering, day by day, with training and massage, how to use each of their limbs. I still drank, but only in the evenings once Lisa was in bed, and no longer to the point of not knowing where I was when I woke in the morning.

Julie slipped away the day I was able to go to the market alone. She left as discreetly as she had arrived.

That was seven years ago, and I don't think I've seen her more than ten times since. Delicacy on her part, embarrassment on mine. We both prefer to act as if those months never happened.

Since then, she's opened a cheesemonger and looks after her goats in Larzac. She seems happy.

Laïvely clears her throat, dragging me out of my thoughts.

I'm standing motionless in the middle of the garage like an idiot, my arms dangling at my sides.

'Lunch is ready!' Babette shouts.

That leaves me with the afternoon to complete all the odd jobs for which she expects me to take responsibility. Babette can sometimes be very old fashioned when it comes to dividing the household chores.

I close the garage door, and it bids me farewell with its particular little cry as I reach the top of the stairs.

It will soon be six in the evening, and I haven't really made any progress. I did put a healthy amount of oil on the hinges, but the door seems to be mocking me and throws out its complaints each time I open or close it. I've observed its mechanisms up close, pricked my ears up at its signature tune and tried to look for the source of the problem, all without reaching any conclusions. Lisa suggests it's some sort of invitation to find Alice and the rabbit, that the door is showing us the way but we're too old to find it. Laïvely laughs tenderly at this idea. The three of us stay there for a while, in the garage, whispering ever so slightly scary stories to each other as we devour a packet of sour strawberry sweets.

From time to time, Babette calls out to me from the top of the steps to find out how I'm getting on.

'I'll be done soon!' I shout back each time, my companions stifling their giggles behind me.

If Babette hears them, she doesn't say anything. We can't spend every Sunday in the world complaining to one another, it's exhausting.

With Lisa now gone, Laïvely chooses to play an old Françoise Hardy album. Sitting on a box, I offer myself a cigarette as I stare into space. I feel good, alone here among the vestiges of my existence. Safe. I don't smoke often – almost never – but I keep a packet hidden behind Lisa's green scooter for moments like this, bitter-sweet, poignant. After all, there are worse places to spend part of the weekend. And life doesn't resemble a drain every day. It sometimes offers you crumbs of happiness that taste like quince and vanilla crumble. It's fanciful to expect anything more. Only fools and idiots do.

The two notes that haven't left me for days suddenly come back to haunt me. I sigh. Tomorrow, maybe, I will eventually be able to extract a theme, a rhythm, a melody.

I crush the cigarette butt with my heel, hide it with the others behind the wheel of a rusty old bike, close the door to the garage, which, this time, seems to snigger at me. I climb the internal staircase, which leads up to the hallway, and switch off the light once I reach the landing.

A strident beep pierces my ear drums.

Below me, behind the glass pane of the door, Laïvely, red in colour, glows in the darkness.

I quickly retrace my footsteps, sorry I have left her behind downstairs. Just as I have almost reached her she suddenly goes out, plunging me into darkness. Carried along by my own momentum, I miss a step as I open the door, my ankle twists and I tumble gracelessly to the floor, where I break my fall with my hands, stunned.

Laughter rings through the room. A laugh without tenderness, a laugh with a perceptible note of raw malice. A laugh tinged with red and black blood, a laugh from the shadows that smells of sulphur and overcooked meat, though I can still make out a few specks of silver. A laugh, I am sure, that doesn't belong to Liv's repertoire.

London

TWENTY YEARS EARLIER

Ellie Zienstein was a petite woman who resembled Joey's agent in *Friends*, feature for feature. She had red, frizzy, dishevelled hair, lips that were hastily painted in bright colours and clashed atrociously with her floral blouses. She gave off the general allure of a tobacco tin, was loudmouthed, had the laugh of a happy donkey, and wore huge cheap rings on each of her fingers … Even in London, where anything goes, she turned heads wherever she went.

She loved Liv's work at the hospital. She often went there to see one of her oldest friends, who was being ravaged by a cancer that would not spare her. However, thanks to the delicate handiwork of Liv, this friend had found a semblance of femininity again. Ellie Zienstein wasn't surprised often, and her convictions were rarely shaken. But her friend's metamorphosis did exactly that.

Ellie was not an agent. She was one of those women who have been blessed with means and contacts, who could allow herself the luxury of impulsive desire and spontaneous tirades, for the simple pleasure of brightening up her day with something other than the sparkle of ice cubes in a glass of gin and tonic. From the very first time they met in the private mansion Ellie owned on a small, discreet street in Kensington, Liv had fallen under her spell.

That evening ocean blues and off-whites mixed with watery greens and aquamarines. The sounds twinkled as they left Liv's mouth, taking flight with the lightness of morning dew. Ellie had completely enchanted her, and I was so captivated by the sonorous and visual union emanating from Liv that I was left incapable of following the threads of the story she was weaving.

Two days later, I had a more precise idea of Ellie's power when the telephone rang and Liv was offered a job as a make-up artist at one of the most famous theatres in the West End, the Lyceum, for the musical *The Lion King*. When she hung up, the joy burst out of her – she let out shrieks more worthy of an American cheerleader at the Super Bowl than a sage English girl. She jumped up and down as she swirled around our little bedroom, leapt on the bed, and finished by crushing me in her arms, short of breath, her face split with a resounding smile, her eyes sparkling with joy. A job on a musical, something she had always dreamt of. *The Lion King* had defined her childhood. She spent the evening whistling 'Hakuna Matata' (out of tune), which I did my best to accompany, clicking along with my fingers.

Ellie could have taken on any role. Cruella, Malevolent, the evil stepmother from Cinderella. For us though, she was a fairy godmother, loving, thoughtful and gentle. She didn't have children, let alone grandchildren, and perhaps in us she found the characters she lacked in real life. However, we brought along the added advantage that she only had to appear when she felt like it, and she could disappear at the first sign of a frown.

Overcome with gratitude, we were ready to bend to her every whim, to anticipate her every wish.

Very quickly, she made us her little protégés, and whilst Liv was doing the make-up at the Lyceum, I had started to play for wealthy individuals who thought it was chic to have a young French man with the air of a nineteenth-century tortured poet about him play in their living room at cocktail hour as little canapés did the rounds. The fact that the young French man in question also had the good taste never to take drugs and never to get drunk, and had the ability to hold a conversation, made them blissfully happy. In the same era, Kate Moss and Johnny Depp were set on destroying their hotel rooms, 'ladettes' were scouring the streets and pubs of London, rock wasn't dead, punk was alive and kicking and the stars were snorting endless lines. Liv and I were anachronisms that melted into the sumptuous and antiquated décor of those beautiful houses nestled around Hyde Park, with their classic elegance and quintessentially British charm.

Soon, we were able to move. We were immediately hooked by the charm of Greenwich. The banks of the Thames, its little streets, the park, Blackheath ... Sure, it took us further from the centre. For some of the people we knew, it was all but an exile, adding a touch more of exoticism to our relationship. Us, we were happy there. The covered markets, the flea markets, the fact that we could reach the West End by water, and the calm of the neighbourhood, all of it was just right for us.

We found a little one-bedroom flat, miniscule and badly insulated, but, as Liv pointed out to me on the first winter evening we spent there, shivering as we curled up for the first time beneath the covers in our first place, so was most London accommodation.

Ellie continued to watch over us, and it was rare that we went more than a week without seeing her. She would summon us to Harrods or The Ritz, the two places she had a predilection for. Occasionally, she would have us over to hers, no fuss, '*sans chichis*', she would say in French with a heavy accent before bursting into laughter, her head thrown back, the wrinkles on her neck twitching, her necklaces lost within them. Facing her, Liv and I, huddled together on a velvet, almond-syrup-coloured chaise longue, looked like two fledglings who had fallen from the nest. She enveloped us in her perfume, her affection and her fancies, taking us away for a weekend to her large family estate, where sheep dotted the fields like innumerable white peas on a green dress, where horses waited in the stables for someone to ride them, where the staff performed a skilfully orchestrated ballet around her and her guests.

One day she came to ours for dinner and exclaimed at how bohemian our home was, said she loved the colourful hangings we had used to hide the damp stains on the walls, and relished the Indian dishes bought that same morning from a stall on the market. She filled the space so much that the flat seemed to shrink around her, her vocal outbursts travelling through the walls and disturbing the Pakistani neighbours. She woke up the baby next door as she left at one in the morning with as much discretion as if it were the middle of the day.

It was to her I owed my first, somewhat serious, composition, a piece commissioned by a radio station to accompany a theatrical creation by an author who was all the rage and whose name I have since forgotten.

Three years quickly flew by. Amy Winehouse had started to ignite Camden. Her gravelly voice put jazz back in the spotlight. Her excesses reminded the whole world how crazy it was to be young, talented and in love. I indulged in a different kind of excess, but I could only agree with that sentiment. There is nothing more crazy and more marvellous than the alchemy of love, talent, and youth.

Téo had been punished for mocking me. He was at the top of the stairs when I fell, and, even in the darkness, the ballet performed by my arms and my legs, flung in every direction, was funnier to him than any late-night, New Year's Eve, cable-channel bloopers reel.

Babette helped me up, Laïvely wedged under my elbow, and sat me down on one of the kitchen chairs. She's trained in first aid and after applying an ice pack that would help avoid any swelling, quickly bandaged my ankle.

The pain now pulses with dull, repetitive strokes, numbing. We watch a film on the TV – a successful French comedy starring Christian Clavier that I have to admit is pretty good. The house is calm, as if it too were numb. Babette is curled up on the sofa, leaving me slumped on an armchair, a footstool keeping my injured leg raised.

She laughs a lot. I like her laugh. It's a mix of the oboe and the flute, with flavours of parmesan and basil. It has autumnal, sumptuous tones. I smile. I would intertwine my fingers with hers, but she's too far away, and the painkiller she forced me to swallow has left me groggy. I never take medicine. I hate it. For this exact reason: it makes me feel like I'm no longer quite myself, like I'm floating just next to my body, entering and leaving it without really controlling the process.

Clavier pulls a stupid face. Babette bursts into laughter.

I watch her.

A cushion beneath her cheek, lying on her side in a ball, she is all curves and softness. My eyes follow the edges of her hips, the fold of her jeans at her waist, the roundness of her firm buttocks. She's sweet, Babette, there's not a bad bone in her. There's a touch of sadness, perhaps, the kind that makes the best clowns. Her skin is damaged, some stretch marks on her stomach, light little scars that tell the story of the difficulty of being a mother. Liv wore the same scars. War wounds, she said proudly, tracing them with her finger.

My leg stiffens. I move it gently and the pain takes me by surprise. I yelp and Babette quickly sits up.

'Are you alright?' she asks me, worried.

'Yeah, yeah.' I smile, rub my calf.

She resumes her initial position, almost infantile, and forgets about it, swallowed up by the screen and the story of the colourful family. I remember the first time we watched a film like this together. I was fascinated by her ability to be extracted from the world. She lived the story, her features reflecting the emotions of all the protagonists in turn. I'm incapable of such a thing. I tend to watch a film analytically, ready to uncover any incoherence, a bad cut, a weakness in the script or the acting. Music is the only thing that swallows me up like the 'seventh art' swallows up my girlfriend. Otherwise, I prefer to maintain my position of observer and critic, and be wary, always a little, of what is being proposed to me.

The two notes are obsessing me once more, the ones I have no clue what to do with. I close my eyes for a moment. In the kitchen Laïvely echoes out, somewhere between a mountain stream and a little trickle of water.

It is ten-thirty pm. Time to go to bed.

Babette ignores her, focused on the film, impenetrable to anything that could disturb her immediate pleasure.

But I seem to detect a light tremble in Laïvely's tone. And I instantly recognise it as the crimson tinge of guilt.

I couldn't get out of bed this morning, the pain was too much. Babette massaged my ankle with a so-called magic cream and brought me a coffee in bed, along with some magazines that were lying around in the living room, before moving the bedside table closer, piled with all the books that I had promised to read a long time ago now. She assured me she would be back at lunchtime to see how I was doing.

Lisa, the silent shadow of our homestead, has already left. I think I felt her warm breath against my cheek, leaving my sleep uninterrupted. Téo did not come up, but I doubt it was shame that was keeping him away.

Laïvely emits comforting little sounds, something between hums and snores. It's almost like she's trying to console me. Or at least, that's the idea she's giving me. I've spent too long with her, and I have to admit that I often lend her thoughts and feelings that a machine, no matter how gifted and intelligent it is, is incapable of having.

I can see myself in the garage, bent over all her components. Or in my studio, my instruments at the ready, computers plugged in, busy searching for the right tone, the perfect note that would bring Liv's voice to life. I rummaged through my memories, watched old video recordings of afternoons out at St James's Park or elsewhere, videos in which you could hear her laughter, her words muffled by the sounds of the road or other voices. Sometimes I had the feeling I was going mad, that I had lost her colours, her scents, for good, that I had lost everything that would allow me to compose her timbre, her laughter, the expression of her joy, her sadness, her fury. Her love.

The project swallowed me whole for months. I composed nothing else, I was incapable. In any case, there was no particular need to earn money. I'd sold our house for a good price (not surprising in the London market), and the profit allowed me to live without worrying about the next day, as long as the next day didn't drag on for too long.

Like Geppetto, I was on a quest for an absolute, which, of course, meant I could only be disappointed.

And then, one day, Laïvely spoke, and the illusion was enough for me to believe that Liv was there, still among us.

Paganism, pantheism, I don't know, I've always swung between the two. But how beautiful are the beliefs of the first tribes – that the spirits of our ancestors are still here, still existing among our daily lives. Why, from my neighbourhood of Paris, could I not be allowed to believe that an object as insignificant as a tube of aluminium stuffed with wires was some sort of incarnation of the soul of the being I loved?

Clearly, if those closest to me had known what I had done, they would have found it unhealthy. I should move on, and maybe, one day, rebuild my life. Oh, they weren't wrong – my life had been well and truly torn apart, there was no doubt about that. But rebuild it? What exactly did they mean by that? Would I have to start over again? From the very beginning? Redo everything? Choose a more sensible livelihood than composing music? Take up studies at a business school or go into medicine? Become a lawyer or a notary? An accountant or a nurse? A gardener or a salesman? Choose a profession that was honourable, with a salary, that was genuine, with crash barriers – unemployment insurance, a pension? Forget being carried along by dreams, melodies, scents and colours to be reinvented … Forget about having your head in the clouds, or elsewhere. In short, forget about being happy.

Yes, rebuild a life. I lacked the desire to do so, and still do. I have not rebuilt anything, even when I reinvented Liv's voice. Because, of course, Laïvely is just a substitute, a pale imitation of Liv. But sometimes, now, she is more real to me that the woman I once shared my life, my bed, with; the woman who took part of my heart with her.

I tap the cylinder as if to reassure her that I'm alright. That is, if an object can be animated by conscious thought and will.

I shake my head gently, try to organise my thoughts. Laïvely has always been an agreeable companion. Sometimes a little intrusive, sure, but agreeable, nonetheless. And I haven't noticed any significant changes in her since the arrival of Babette and Téo. So, suppose Liv's soul were enclosed in her sturdy metal walls, why would she show the slightest discontent now? Has something happened that I've missed? Could it be the product of something that has escaped me? And why take it out on me? It would be more logical to attack Babette if she perceived her as a rival.

There's a taste of chicken-noodle soup in my mouth, and taupe and pistachio stains dance in front of my eyes. But no matter how hard I listen, not a single sound comes to meet this strange mixture of senses. Except for Laïvely's snoring, so weak that it could even be my own breath, which I am mistaking for hers.

The image of the rabbit is super-imposed on the backdrop of colours in my mind. He has lost his pocket watch and is staring at me, frightened. The squeak of the garage door now echoes through the silence like a scream. I open my eyes, my heart is pounding.

Laïvely flashes emerald green, reassuring.

I smile and lower my eyelids. And then, nothing.

London

It was no longer the London of twenty years earlier. The years had flown by in a flighty farandole, and Liv and I danced to our own rhythm.

Our dear Ellie was ageing, badly. The gin and the slim cigarettes she was fond of eventually demanded payment for the services they had rendered. She coughed a lot. Sometimes she spat up blood – discreetly, into her white batiste handkerchiefs, tainting them vermillion. I shuddered. I'd always been able to decipher Death beneath the embellishments it took on when it decided to appear in masquerade. It was only Liv's that was a real surprise.

Ellie then, was getting old. But that didn't stop her treating us, as always, with her signature combination of condescension and love. She was definitely more attached to her three King Charles Spaniels than she was to any other human, but that in no way stopped her from devoting her generosity, her advice and her tenderness to us.

Thanks to her, we had work, and good work. We'd left Greenwich for a pink house on a mews near

Paddington Station, a house that we had bought. I liked losing myself in Paddington Station. The hustle and bustle that reigned over it inspired me more than that of any other train station I had ever found myself in; Saint-Lazare, Nice-Ville, Montparnasse, Lyon-Perrache – none of them were quite like Paddington. The house too, was just right for us. It was the Pink Panther's, Liv had decided the day we visited it. The interior was, indeed, a little dated, as in the films of that aged panther, and the façade, well, it was the same pink colour as the feline in the cartoons. We got into the habit of walking up the stairs on our tiptoes, leaning forwards slightly, humming the unforgettable theme tune. In front of the house, in the big, bright-blue planters, Liv had planted daffodil, narcissus and tulip bulbs, whose sprouts she spent hours preening, waiting with ever more impatience to see them bloom in spring. My piano furnished our living room, which was otherwise almost empty. We were not frugal, no, but the desire to possess didn't seem to be a part of our DNA. At the request of our small group of friends – including Laila, the costume designer we'd stayed in touch with after the *Picture of Dorian Gray* fiasco and who complained of a bad back – we finally acquired a big, second-hand, worn leather Chesterfield sofa. Our books were piled up without rhyme or reason on the salvaged shelves, which were mostly made up of empty cases of wine that we had arranged as we could, balanced precariously on top of one another. In our bedroom was a large bed, a quilt that was never tucked in, pillows and cushions strewn on the floor, and a dressmaker's mannequin holding up Liv's numerous stoles and scarves, each more colourful than the last. Years earlier, in Greenwich Market, I had unearthed a gramophone that now presided on an old sewing table. We'd play old records on it from time to time, but we had to get out of bed to set it up and would always end up gently arguing about who the task would fall to when none of us wanted to leave the warmth of the sheets. In the mornings, Liv sipped her milky tea from a mug bearing Princess Diana's face, and I drank my espresso from a tiny grey bowl, a memory of a trip to Greece we had gone on a few years earlier during a sweltering September. On that trip Liv wore a huge hat to protect her delicate skin from the sun, and we swam naked, during the night, in a glassy Mediterranean. Never had love been so tender as it was during that September, when we rediscovered our bodies in the heat of the sheets, on the tiles of our little white-walled house by the sea.

Our Paddington house then, harboured our memories, sheltered our casualness, and was home to our life – in which we never projected ourselves forwards further than the next minute, further than the caress that was about to come. In the evenings, I played for Liv. Old standards from the 1960s, jazz, Philip Glass. She was particularly fond of Tchaikovsky, some Chopin nocturnes, Art Tatum. And Satie, always.

We were happy, but we would have been happy anywhere. Our love was beyond comment, beyond question, beyond doubt. It enveloped us, kept us prisoner, willing and consenting inmates. The idea of escaping this bubble would never have crossed our minds. To do what? To go where? To other bodies? To taste other kisses? That would all have been futile, when Liv was the woman, all women, the lover, the mistress, the sweetheart, the sister, the wife and so much more. I don't know if it was her ability to make up others that made her so adept at playing with her own masks, but Liv knew how to be multiple, that much was clear, and I never missed out on anything while I was with her.

Out of amusement to start with, and then out of passion, she started learning French. She sang Piaf with a deep voice as she did the dishes, ironed with Barbara, 'La Chanteuse de minuit', and as we cycled through London's parks, she belted out Gainsbourg at passers-by. She had a boundless admiration for Jane

Birkin, and for a time tried to imitate her style, although unsuccessfully, as their bodies had little in common. Their voices were far from similar too, Liv's English accent when she spoke the language of Molière was much less marked than that of her compatriot.

At night, under our blankets, we told stories, like children trying to frighten each other. I used to make her laugh out loud every time I tried to pronounce the word 'trout' correctly, or perform the cock-a-doodle-doo, which is nothing like the cock-a-doodle-doo heard in the backyards on the other side of the Channel. I amused myself by asking her to repeat after me that *'les chaussettes de la duchesse étaient séches'*. As the hours flew by, we invented a language with golden edges and clear harpsichord notes, and that suited us fine.

And then Liv became pregnant.

Ten days have passed. I'm still limping a little, more because I'm seeking sympathy and trying to avoid everything than out of real pain. Babette is not fooled, but she doesn't say anything.

Spring is struggling to take hold. It's drizzly, day after day. The only touches of blue are those of Alice's dress on the façade, Lisa's irises in her large, beautiful, serious face. My daughter smiles sometimes, as if a cloud were brushing gently across her lips. She barely speaks. But she slips her hand into mine beneath the table, and the pressure of her fingers tells me just how much love she has for me.

The two notes that have been tormenting me have finally gone to play outside. I didn't know what to do with them and so they deserted me, and that's quite normal. One cannot work miracles, and one cannot expect two notes to haunt one forever. They gave me a chance, before giving up and going to sing elsewhere. To hold a grudge against them would be futile. With them have gone the dark pinks and the touch of crimson that pleased me, the scent of lavender and cherry blossom. Maybe they will come back.

When Babette and Téo moved in, we changed the layout of the rooms. Babette, with her tracksuits and jeans, floated into the bedroom that I had first occupied alone, and Téo invaded the room on the second floor that until his arrival was home to my music studio, a floor above Babette and me. That way we'll have more privacy, declared his mother on the day of the big upheaval, as I have always secretly called the day they moved in. They arrived with their Ikea furniture (not much), their trinkets, their posters, their tastes and their colours. It was quite a happy day, when I think about it. There was noise everywhere, a cacophony that tasted of sauerkraut and *tarte tropézienne*, experimental music played in a cave lit up by candlelight. We walked up and down the stairs. We laughed. We also broke a few glasses, but nobody cared. Evening came, and everyone tried to find their bearings on that first night under a strange roof, me just as much as the others. The shadows drawn by Bab's wardrobe were not the same shadows I was used to. In the dark, I stubbed my big toe against her little rattan armchair, a relic of her student days when she moved to Paris from her provincial home (Toulon, in this case, where we have been planning to go ever since, without ever carrying our promises through, the city only ever evoking military marches and the smell of churros fried beneath Frida Kahlo colours).

Laïvely laughed with us, at least that's how it seemed to me. I have very little memory of her presence in those days. Maybe she was more discreet, perhaps she didn't leave my studio, I don't know. What is certain is that since then she's never left my side. I even take her to the bathroom with me. As I shower, her humming, together with the sound of the water that washes over my body, reminds me of the laughter of Our Lady of the Bells.

When did it first happen? It was after Babette had moved in – that's the only thing I'm sure of. If she hadn't been living with us, I would never have reacted as I did. But the day I became aware of what I was doing is burnt into my memory.

It was a Thursday. The kids were in school. Babette and I were alone in the house. We had just made love. Babette called me from the shower. Our bathroom led off our bedroom. Laïvely took pride of place on my bedside table, an eyesore Babette had brought with her, but that was so much more functional, she told me – with its plywood surface pierced by a hole through which passed the electrical wires that fed the radio-alarm, the phone, and other devices – so much more practical than the child's high-chair that had been ripped from the room of relics and had, until Babette arrived, fulfilled the bedside role.

I joined Babette in the shower, and we picked up our caresses beneath the hot water that ran down our backs. And it was then that I heard it. Liv's laugh. That crystalline laugh. Unique. That laugh that capsized me each time it reached my ears. That laugh I once sought to provoke no matter the cost. With silly antics and feeble imitations of Tony Blair and Margaret Thatcher. Even Mr Bean. That laugh captivated me. And it continued to have this effect. I froze mid-kiss. I pulled back. Babette waited a moment, opened her eyes, interrogated me with a glance. Distressed, I left the shower without a word, incapable of formulating what even I could not understand.

'Stan, what's wrong?' she had asked me, suddenly worried.

I sat on the bidet, one of the last random survivors of a world I had reigned over before Babette had arrived.

'I … I don't know. Vertigo?'

She turned off the water. The laughing stopped. I screwed my eyelids shut, pinched my lips, held back my tears, my sobs. I was haunted.

Once we were dressed we went down to the kitchen. Babette made a point of making me eat a slice of bread with honey, a trusted remedy for drops in blood pressure, blood sugar, and who knows what else. She mothered me, laughing, happy with herself for having exhausted me, proud of her achievement. I let her do and say as she pleased. But within me that laugh echoed, the laughter of Our Lady of the Bells, of a triangle, of round, firm raindrops with bluish outlines. And the honey took on the ashy taste of over-toasted bread.

A year, more or less, has gone by since then. I've always managed to avoid having sex in the bathroom. Or to make sure that Laïvely isn't hanging around. But I have to admit that for some time now, tender moments between Babette and me have become fewer and fewer. And even rarer are the times when I really, truly let myself go.

Am I indifferent to Babette? To her feelings, to her happiness? No, surely not. But little by little, I feel myself drifting, getting further away, as if I were on a conveyor belt that, slowly, was dragging me towards a departure gate for a flight to nowhere. Slowly but surely. And more and more often, I drown myself in that bell-like laughter as the hot water trickles over my skin, the shower head intertwining its melody with Laïvely's. Because, after that first time, all I could think of was repeating the experience, to assure myself that I had neither dreamt it, nor been the victim of a daydream, in the way I had as a child, when I believed I saw Dagobert disappear behind a hedge, trotting away from me, although he had already been gone for many months.

I play two chords on the piano. Loud. I want to believe that I still hold my destiny in my hands. I want to.

London

Liv, pregnant, was radiant. It was as if she were born for maternity. Her body rounded out harmoniously, and she suffered nothing of morning sickness, dizziness, shortness of breath or mood swings. She was happy, her voice reminded me of little raspberry tartlets served with single cream, and everything was in pastel colours. When she spoke, it sounded as if a flute was taking precedence over all other instruments – a subtle flute whose sound was only a little lower than normal.

She continued to work, unfazed, swinging her stomach and her blossoming hips across the pavements of the city, carving out a natural passageway in the crowd that thronged the Strand. Now she preferred orange or apple-green scarves, flared gypsy skirts, big, grey mohair jumpers. Her hair, which she had cut short, swept across her forehead and her little porcelain ears and fell into her eyes, where I detected a light that I had not seen before. The pink barrette's task was now easier, and it no longer seemed to complain.

I composed, a lot, and left our house very little. In Mothercare, we had bought a cot that looked like a cosy cocoon. In Greenwich Market, which we continued to visit regularly, we found a wooden mobile where old boats and airplanes from another century danced together. Everything found its place in the corner of our large bedroom, where a screen with birds of paradise in faded colours divided the room into two unequal parts.

We didn't wish to know the sex of the baby. We researched names – and invented them too. Rose? Dahliette? Douglen? Elizabeth? Martin? Philip was put to the side very quickly, judged too royal. The same was done with Diana. We hesitated between old French names, snubbed Mickaëls and Kevins without dwelling on them. On the piano I played light melodies with spellbinding refrains. Liv sung, a needle in hand – she had discovered a taste for embroidery. Laila mocked us, saying we were the perfect image of a timeless couple, almost accusing us of being old fashioned.

Thanks to Ellie, I had composed the music for my first film, a re-enactment of the Battle of Waterloo for the BBC. Since then, I'd had a steady stream of commissions, everything from cable television adverts to variety show jingles, documentaries and TV series. We hadn't changed our lifestyle, and our names remained unknown to the general public; we were happy, and we watched Liv's belly grow with a strange emotion.

And then came the obvious. Lisa, she would be Lisa. The letters that formed the name were taken from each of ours, like a confirmation of our unbreakable bond. From the day we decided, we had no doubts whatsoever. Not about the name, nor about the sex of the child that was about to come. You'd have thought that the little girl had told us who she was herself, from the womb. Liv set herself about embroidering those four letters on little baby grows, white cotton sleeping bags, swaddles. The perfect balance of the name enchanted us. I wrote a four-beat lullaby. Liv came up with the lyrics. The house took on colours of pudding, scents of freshly cut herbs, and hummed gently, even its pink seeming to soften under the torrential rains of that spring.

'We could have dinner at the restaurant, what do you think?'

Babette is overflowing with optimism. I feel like it must be some sort of anniversary, when she moved in, probably. But last spring, the sun wasn't lacking, the first warm spells were making our cheeks rosy, and our shorts were getting shorter and shorter. This year, only the rain accompanies us. I shiver. Laïvely has been particularly silent today. Earlier I played some old lullabies with just two fingers, those I'd written for Lisa's birth. Simple notes, sweet, the kind one hums without thinking, a familiar perfume in my nostrils, L'Heure bleue by Guerlain, perhaps, with the tastes of milk roll and a block of chocolate on my tongue. I don't feel like going out. Night has already fallen. I don't like the yellowed halo emitted by the lampposts at the bottom of the street, the hospital-white aura of those on the boulevard. But Babette smiles at me, and in her eyes I see the light that used to shine there when we first started seeing each other, during our first dinners at the Chinese restaurant on the corner, where she would tell me about how she had come to Paris, about her first flat, whose walls were so thin she could hear her neighbour sneeze, yet had never even met him on the stairs.

'OK, let me fetch a warmer jumper and we'll go.'

She stops herself from jumping up and down on the spot like an excited child, and it's my turn to smile. Yes, an evening in our little Chinese restaurant, abandoned for too long, a beer, a stir-fry … a taste of normality. I embrace her, kiss her. She rubs her nose against mine, an Eskimo kiss, another way of saying 'I love you', bypassing words. I give in to her, squeeze her a little tighter. Then I let her go with one last peck.

In our room, Laïvely flickers, her light a sickly green. I decide to ignore her. Surely she's not planning on accompanying us to the restaurant?

But when I try to open the wardrobe door, it resists. I pull a little harder. Nothing. I wiggle the handle. Nothing happens. I step back and study the stubborn piece of furniture. There's nothing original about this classic, Ikea-crafted wardrobe. Two white doors, a handle to turn. I'm not even sure you can close the lock with a key, and, if there is one, I've never seen it.

I feel something like a breath on my back. I shudder. I squeeze my nose, a sneeze tickling my nostrils before fading away.

'Hurry up! Are you ready? I'm waiting,' Babette shouts from the ground floor.

'I'm coming.'

I try again. The door opens without even a creak. I study it, perplexed. I close it again. I open it again. And again. Ten times over. Nothing. No problem. I must have dreamt it.

I grab my old woollen jumper, camel-coloured, brought back from a trip to Scotland, where Liv and I had drunk too much whisky, eaten too much salmon, and seen too many lochs. You can't always escape the clichés. As was expected, it had rained non-stop, and I feared that mushrooms would end up sprouting between my toes. In the evenings, we took refuge in pubs that were overheated by frenzied flames. The men spoke loudly, their accents rendering the language indecipherable. Everything was adorned in gold and perfumed with the scent of chestnuts. Liv kissed me full on the lips – she smelt of alcohol and smoke from the chimneys.

The wardrobe door slams shut, just missing my fingers. I jump back, my pulse racing.

A tiny laugh. I turn sharply to the threshold of the bedroom, convinced I will discover my daughter standing there.

Deserted.

The laugh sounds out again.

Laïvely flickers. Green and red. Like a bloody Christmas tree.

Babette babbles. Her arm passes through mine, she advances with a light step along the boulevard in the direction of the restaurant. The heat of her body against mine. I feel its firmness, its suppleness. A vague desire comes over me and gives me the powerful sensation of being alive. Violently. Briefly. Babette doesn't notice a thing as we make our way along the pavement, and I try to shake off the fleeting, dazzling effect. It's the kind of urge that I haven't experienced in a long while, and by the time we've made it to the restaurant it's piercing the fog I feel I have been attempting to move through in the last few weeks. A fog that has insidiously taken up residence around me and threatens to engulf me completely.

'Your hands are cold,' Babette gasps as my fingers brush her neck as I help her take off her coat.

'Yeah, sorry. Considering it's April, we're way off the mark. It's like November out there.'

The boss bustles around us, all bows and smiles. He doesn't speak a word of French, or, at least, he pretends not to. But we always have the impression of being welcomed by an old friend when he sits us at our favourite table. Months can pass without us coming, yet he never forgets which one it is.

Babette thanks him with a smile and immerses herself in the menu. She'll have the pineapple chicken, the steamed prawn dumplings, a Chinese beer. But she'll pretend that she could be tempted, maybe this time, by something else.

'Have you decided?' she asks me eventually, lifting her nose from the menu.

She is beautiful, in that moment, Babette. I notice that she has even delicately applied some make-up, something she almost never does. I lean over to brush one of her blonde curls back from her face. She takes advantage of this movement to leave a kiss on my palm, stroke her cheek against my hand for an instant. She smiles.

'The same as always,' I reply.

She's not the only one to have her rites and rituals. For me it will be grilled dumplings, Peking duck, and Cantonese rice, just for the pleasure of the sounds the words make. And beer.

The boss materialises at our table as if by magic, his nose already in his pad. Babette reels off the numbers associated with the dishes. He nods frantically before heading back to the kitchen, where he shouts a few commands that we cannot understand.

'Have you noticed the wardrobe door is stuck?'

I can't help asking her the question. I've started to think I'm imagining things, a result of secluding myself in my studio, on the lookout for notes that escape me more and more often.

'No … Why?'

'Nothing … Well, yeah. I had all the trouble in the world opening it just now.'

Babette shrugs her shoulders, plays with her chopsticks. 'I don't know what to tell you. Maybe some clothes got stuck?'

'Maybe, yeah.'

'Did I tell you Marie's met someone? She's on cloud nine.'

And off she goes, telling me all about the receptionist at work's latest fling. At nearly sixty years old, Marie continues to dress and behave like a teenager. Always vibrant and smiley, always in a good mood, her bursts of laughter break up the continuous roar of the children who jump into the swimming pool and splash around. I like her laugh a lot. She's a blend of rhubarb and wild fennel with hints of violet in bloom. It envelops you like the softest of robes. Marie has spent her whole life looking for love, finding it and losing it like someone who misplaces their keys.

'Jean-Marc is really lovely – we had a chat yesterday when he came to pick her up. He's a removal man, divorced, a grandfather. But, most importantly, it seems like he really loves her.'

'Well, that's good. She deserves to be happy, Marie.'

'As do we all,' hits back Babette, who doesn't see why having lost a son, won a pitched battle against breast cancer and lived alone for more than fifteen years gives Marie any greater right to happiness.

I don't pick her up on it. She's like that, Babette. Generous, but rough around the edges. After all, she too has battled. And her struggles are no less deserving than those of her sisters in arms.

'I've been called into the school again,' she sighs as she stuffs a fork full of chicken into her mouth.

'Ah, really?'

'Yeah. Téo got into a fight at breaktime.'

That a teenager so sluggish he casts doubt on the classification of living things into vertebrates and invertebrates could be capable of such an act amazes me. But I keep my thoughts to myself.

'With Mathias. Even though they've been friends since they were eleven.'

'A girl thing?'

'Could be. I'll know more tomorrow. They didn't want to tell me anything over the phone.'

It's not that I don't like Téo, but more that I don't feel anything towards him. We live under the same roof, that's all. As long as he doesn't bother Lisa, as long as he leaves her alone, everything's fine. I couldn't care less if he gets good marks, joins the army or becomes a table tennis champion. Something that, evidently, I cannot share with his mother.

'Let me know what they say. It's frustrating.'

'It is … By the way, I've booked some days off in the spring holidays. Shall we go away?'

I stiffen. We never go anywhere. I never feel the need. Worse even, I dread it. It's as if in moving away from the Rabbit Hole I take the risk of seeing it disappear forever.

'Hmmm…'

Babette continues, in her eyes the plan apparently agreed upon.

'I found a nice campsite, in Landes. Téo could try out surfing. And it would be good for us to have a change of scenery. Breathe in the ocean air rather than chlorine. Personally, I don't see why we shouldn't.'

'When do the holidays fall?'

She swallows her sigh. It's no use complaining – men are made in such a way that they leave the women to take care of these kinds of contingencies.

Even dads. And when the men in question are also artists, then … well, it would be ridiculous to expect them to remember such unimportant details.

'In three weeks' time. I'll show you the campsite when we get home. You'll see, it's great. They rent out little bungalows right on the water, it looks magical.'

'Doesn't it always rain in Landes at this time of year?'

'No more than anywhere else, I don't think.'

'OK, well, we'll have a look.'

But I already know that I won't go. I'll pretend to have a composition to deliver, an urgent job, whatever. I don't want to leave the Rabbit Hole. And even less so Laïvely, who would have no reason to join us on the trip. I'm suddenly aware that the only explanation I have for my decision to stay behind is this slightly unhealthy attachment. From now on, though, I do need to keep my eye on her. Paradoxically, the more she intervenes in our lives, as she has done recently, the more I have the feeling that she's drifting away from me. Or rather, that Liv's voice is telling me stories I don't recognise. Because Liv was all tenderness and kindness, and Laïvely seems to be taking an evil turn. Hateful. Uncontrollable. Unless I'm losing my mind. Laïvely has never been more than what is asked of her: a good object that breaks up the solitude. She's electronic, a few notes, a search engine. How could she respond emotionally to any situation?

When we get home, she is deep in silence. The children have gone to bed without a fuss. Babette goes upstairs to check that they're sleeping, and I hang around in the living room, using my ankle as an excuse to let her do it. The truth is otherwise. I'm afraid that if I cross the threshold into my daughter's room, I won't be able to leave again, and I will stay there the whole night, drinking and watching her sleep. After she was born, I spent every night like this, minus the alcohol. Liv would find me curled up in a ball at the foot of the cot, sleep having finally overcome me. Lisa, her big eyes open, smiling up at the angels on the ceiling as if it were she who was watching over her father, and not the other way around.

Babette does not come back down. She must be showering, getting ready for bed. And waiting for me.

London

Lisa is here. She arrived on her due date. Liv gave birth to her at home, barely a scream. Mother and child are doing well. Our bubble has grown to welcome this wonder, this perfect little bundle, with fingers so long and slim, and eyelashes whose shadows dance on her cheeks. Her skin is soft, her head smooth. Her toothless mouth swallows her mother's breast greedily. Laila came to visit us – she declared herself nauseous at all the family happiness. Ellie, hospitalised, has sent us gifts that are far too big for the little girl: a rocking horse that even I find giant and am scared to get onto, a Paddington bear the size of an eight-year-old that we have no idea where to put because it terrorises Lisa so much, roses galore for Liv, who finds their scent too heady, and even a miniature piano that Lisa definitely won't use for another two or three years.

It was a mild summer, the heatwave had struck elsewhere, and we walked along the paths of St James's Park, down the slopes of Greenwich and slowly along the Serpentine, pushing an antique pram that Liv had found in a charity shop. It must have been from the

1960s, but it resembled the pram of a little prince, just like the one that appeared in photos in which Diana and Charles also starred, and that was enough to convince her of the soundness of this out-of-the-ordinary purchase. The pram, quite weighty, required all my strength to hoist it back into our living room after each outing. Then we had to swerve and spin around it, as if on a crazy merry-go-round. It served as a place to leave whatever we had in our hands if a cry from our daughter tore us from our initial destination.

Lisa was an easy baby, docile. Very quickly, she started to sleep through the night. She particularly liked bath time, which took place in our big washbasin, where she played at sending the water flying in every direction with her ferocious little feet. We came out of it as soaked as she was, and we quickly got into the habit of undressing to bathe her.

Liv didn't go back to work in September. I composed frantically when she went into the city with Lisa, leaving me with a small span of time in which I could pull from my piano the most violent, high-pitched chords without fear of disturbing anyone. My works then, were devoid of all gentleness, rather they expressed the violence of the feelings that I felt for my daughter. She had ravished my heart, and now I understood, physically, the significance of such a phrase. My clients were astonished by my work, but they were madly in love with it and found it now had an indefinable touch that was previously missing. If I had to give that *je-ne-sais-quoi* a name, I would have spoken of completeness. For the first time in my life, I felt whole. Justified. Legitimate. Forgotten were the years of solitude, of mixing colours, scents, and flavours, organising them in an attempt to make sense of the world that surrounded me. Gone were the doctors' surgeries, nurses, the diagnoses of my childhood, the illnesses whispered among adults, parental worries, and the attempts to fit into moulds that were so profoundly foreign to me. All those who were not us were wiped off the face of the Earth. Now I had a duty, a genuine task. I was a father. Lisa depended on me like no one ever had before. Everything took on a new depth, as if my love story with her mother was nothing but a long prelude to me slowly waking up to the world. A world that I adorned with lights, colours and sounds that would please this child, this miracle, this fairy. She was my saviour, my passion, my redemption.

Through her, Liv and I became one, eternal. We were the perfect trinity, the only thing that made sense.

So, Lisa grew, she spoke her first words, took her first steps, experienced her first sorrows. My music changed once more – it became softer, a cocoon made to protect her from all the dangers of the world, those I could perceive and others I could not even imagine. She sat upright at the foot of the piano, her serious little face lifted towards me, as if hypnotised by the music. And I played and I played again, and she never tired of it.

Liv started working again. Lisa stayed with me. If Liv suffered from that separation, she never told me about it. She left around eleven o'clock to prepare the faces that were to appear in the matinée. Sometimes she got back very late, and I only discovered her again in the morning, her sleeping body against mine. I woke her up by making love to her softly, in silence, joining myself with her to give her my strength, my love, my tenderness, everything that could fulfil her. She would open her eyes in a moan of pleasure, closing her arms around me, and we would cling on to those precious moments of intimacy and togetherness. Then Lisa would call out, and we would have breakfast, share the first laughs of the day, the first tears too, sometimes, if the chocolate was too hot, a toy was too far away, or simply on a whim. The three of us spent the morning together. It always passed by too quickly. Then Liv would nibble something on the go as I prepared Lisa's lunch, which I would share with her later. And the rest of the day was ours.

I went to the park this afternoon. Lisa came with me. The sky, miraculously, was bright. I felt like getting some air; my daughter joined me.

We sat on the grass for a moment, watching the people who were around us, living. Joggers, groups of teenagers clumped together on a bench, each one glued to their smartphone. We imagined their lives, their families, their dreams and their illusions. Lisa has always been very good at this game; one we've been playing since she was tiny. At first, she was too young to play opposite me, to take my cues, so I would go on for hours about lives I knew nothing of. That afternoon, once again, she listened to me, serious, concentrated. She nodded in agreement when the story seemed right, wrinkled her brow at a digression or an incoherence on my part. If that woman was a retired teacher, then the book she was reading had to be a classic romance novel, because I'd made her a spinster. Lisa was convinced: it could only be *Madame Bovary*, or at the very least *The Devil in the Flesh*. But definitely not a Camille Laurens. An Alice Ferney?

Why not, yes, she conceded with a little pout, not completely convinced. If that man was a spurned lover, why was he suddenly smiling at the young girl walking past with her dog? Reflex, of course. Lisa shrugged her shoulders without bothering to answer. I was just a fool, ponderous, a guy who knew nothing about those things, she seemed to be thinking. So, I smiled and watched the miniscule, playful clouds dance for a moment, and said nothing else.

When we get back, Téo is eating a snack in the kitchen. Lisa disappears into her bedroom after leaving a quick peck on my cheek and whispering a 'thanks Dad' in my ear.

Laïvely is on top of the work surface. Switched off, it looks like.

'Is Laïvely not working?'

I lift her up, turn her around, but the object remains inanimate, nothing more than a tube and wires, nothing interesting.

'Dunno.'

But by the way he is avoiding my eyes, Téo is telling me more than he wants to.

'What have you done?' My voice verges on an animalistic growl. Laïvely's silence drills into my ears. I couldn't bear to lose her. I put her down gently.

'Nothing!' the teenager defends himself, and tries to make his way over to the door to leave.

I block his path, square up to him with my full height.

'What have you DONE?'

'NOTHING!'

I grab him by the arms, shake him.

'Stop lying! Tell me – NOW!'

He cries out in pain, fear lights up in his eyes and his facial features break down.

'Stan…' he murmurs in a tiny voice, the desire to fight having left him.

But the blood is pounding through my ears, I can't hear anything anymore, I literally see red.

'What have you DONE? You IDIOT!'

And I shake, and shake, Téo's hair slaps across his face, his head is bobbing around like a rag doll's, and his cries are suffocated by my anger. Only one phrase is running in a loop through my mind, the question that he is not responding to. What have you done? What have you done?

A high-pitched scream tears me from my prey.

'Stan!'

It's Babette, who I hadn't even heard come in. Her son takes advantage of the interruption to slip away and escape. He gallops up the stairs, the door to his room slams shut.

Babette, horrified, pale, stares at me as if seeing me for the first time. On the work surface, Laïvely twinkles green, as if nothing has happened.

Babette leaves the room and heads upstairs to join her son.

Laïvely lets out a little sigh. Of pleasure. Hadn't I just proved to her how much I care for her? To the point of physically attacking a child, because, despite what he thinks, Téo is nothing but a kid. Did she knowingly pretend to be broken? Did she anticipate the rage I would feel? Did I imagine the teenager's evasive stare? I don't know, I don't know anymore.

I shake myself off, move forwards, reach my hand out towards her, pull it back. What will I find if I touch her? The beat of a heart? The warmth of flesh?

I collapse into a chair at the kitchen table, my head in my hands. What am I becoming?

Then I get up with a leap and make my way over to Laïvely. This has gone on long enough. That's it. This thing is driving me crazy.

But just as I am about to grab her, the cupboard door swings open and slams into my face. I wobble backwards, hold my nose in a futile attempt to protect it from the searing pain that's already gripping it. Between the stars that dance in front of my eyes I make out Laïvely's light. A light that has turned blood red.

And then that laughter, that laughter that sounded out in the garage after I fell down the stairs, sounds out again. I freeze on the spot.

London

Lisa discovered the countryside, the sea. We went on holiday. She had just turned four years old. Not too much earlier, Laila had moved to Dorset boasting to whoever wanted to listen about the countryside charm, its green valleys, the purity of the air, the joy of hearing a cockerel sing out from the neighbour's farm, thatched roofs, low-ceilinged rooms and cosy fireplaces (she had not yet lit hers, the season didn't lend itself, but my God, it would certainly happen when autumn made its swift appearance). We had chosen a bed and breakfast not too far from hers, in Lyme Regis. We wandered up and down the beach, had lunch in a pub on Broad Street; we struck up a rhythm and developed habits as if we were never going to return from that place. Lisa had a pair of red wellington boots with white polka dots, and she jumped in the puddles that the sea left behind when it drew back out. She learned that the little boats did not have legs, that dinosaurs had once really existed, but no longer did, that things, people, animals even, disappeared sometimes, something that plunged her into abysses of perplexity.

Liv found a new lease of life. She'd worked too much these last few months, her notoriety only growing over the years. She'd lost weight, and I was happy to watch her stuff herself with fish and chips swimming in vinegar, scones accompanied by Devonshire cream, strange puddings that made me wrinkle my nose. For breakfast we spread raspberry jam on thick pieces of bread that we toasted at will. We drunk sugary tea at all hours. We took a nap at the same time as our daughter. We made love at midday before sinking into sleep. We had dinner early, every other day with Laila, at her place or elsewhere. The former costume designer had started to form a little circle whose members might never become her friends, as they couldn't avoid looking at the London girl who had washed up on their shores with a certain suspicion, but who offered her an illusion of a social life. She was not the first to come here. Often, after two or three years, these new-age country-dwellers would take the road back to the big city, opting for Exeter when they didn't want to move away from the coast. So, the locals would see them less and less, then not at all. Growing attached to them, therefore, was perceived by most as a waste of time. The most welcoming to new arrivals were the most recent migrants, themselves searching for roots, links, anything at all that would make these people, whether they landed from Leeds or Kraków, anything but strangers.

In this motley group there were fishermen, a boat painter, the owner of an antique shop in the neighbouring village, as well as a veteran who had a shop that was difficult to define – as much a hardware store as it was naval supplies. Their English was different to that which I was used to in London, and I discovered new expressions, new notes that until then had remained unknown. For me, those two weeks in Lyme Regis had the taste of Sunday roast potatoes, the scent of jasmine and the golden-brown hues of a Turner. In my head a harpsichord played bright, luminous harmonies, sometimes accompanied by a grumpy oboe.

One day when Liv and Laila went for a girls' day out, taking the little one with them, I stayed alone with David, a funny guy whose physical features put one in mind of Captain Haddock, with a voice that was too soft for his lungs, and an eternally childlike gaze. David, well into his fifties then, had swindled his way around a little of the world before establishing himself in Lyme Regis ten years earlier. Seduced by the place, he had never left. He had a small, gloomy and cluttered shop where one could find everything, especially something you were not looking for. Dusty old sextants rubbed shoulders with state-of-the-art remote-control cars, transistors that were already out of fashion in the 1970s were elbow to elbow with ultramodern turntables. His dainty fingers couldn't resist anything that contained wires and electronic components. He repaired capricious washing machines, deficient coffee machines and computers on strike, all with the same ease. His hands drifted and floated over the broken device for a few minutes, to a rhythm of their own. Then they landed and slowly started to caress the beast. Once it had been tamed, the operation itself was possible. David was then completely immersed in a universe in which he reigned supreme and uncontested. However long it took to carry out the repair, he did not interrupt the process, ever, and didn't lift his head until the operation was finished. Then, he would smile his childlike smile, tap the healed machine and serve himself a glass of water. Once he had finished drinking, he would pick up the thread of the story that had been interrupted by his work from exactly where he had left it, as if he had just woken up from anaesthesia. For my part, I was able to quietly observe his fingers perform their hypnotising ballet almost without breathing.

That day, when I met David in his shop, he was

already occupied. He didn't lift his head when I entered, so I watched him dissect a connected speaker. When he'd finished, I had the impression of hearing the speaker let out a sigh of relief.

'There you are my beauty,' concluded David, patting the speaker with tenderness. 'Just like new. How's it going?' he asked as he turned towards me after putting down his glass of water.

'Aquamarine, reeds scraping against a zinc gutter and pecan tart,' I responded.

I had told David about my bizarre associations, which, throughout my existence so far, rather than allow me to make friends with my contemporaries, had instead distanced me from them.

He scratched his beard. 'A lot of reeds?'

'No, not too many,' I responded after thinking about it.

'Ah, you're alright then, just a passing inconvenience. You must be suffering from the humidity at Bridget's. Her bed and breakfast is cute, but the sea air seeps into the whole house. And the street is gloomy.'

I smiled at being so well understood

'Tell me about the speaker.'

'Myriam? She's still young, but I don't think she's happy at home. She's letting herself die slowly.'

David's animism responded to mine. Or rather, my strange form of synaesthesia, which left many specialists in rationality speechless, found in his animism a reassuring double.

He spoke to me, then, about Myriam, whose breakdown he thought came from her owner's bad taste: they were trying to make her play punk music, when her components clearly indicated that she would prefer baroque.

How did he know?

He showed me the coloured wires in the machine; it seemed at first glance that they were all the same, as with every gadget assembled on the other side of the world at a lower cost. But that was not the case. A nano-millimetre difference in the cut made each of them unique beings and explained their likes and dislikes. He pulled out a blue wire, then a yellow one. I leaned over, not able to discern any difference between them. Then, with a finger, he indicated where to look. The yellow wire didn't seem to have been cut like the blue. He nodded. I had found the answer. Then he pulled the others out. Some came from the same roll of wire, others from completely different batches. Each one told a story that was its own. None had lived, or would ever live, the same life. In these infinite clones, David knew how to recognise the slightest nuance, even the most imperceptible.

He spoke for a long time, telling me strange things, stories of electronic networks that seemed to be gifted with autonomy, inexplicable breakdowns, lights that amused themselves by turning on and off without anyone even touching a switch. His language, rich without being technical, opened up a world of tales and legends from a dimension that I had not known until now. He evoked sounds, noises, sighs even, let out by transistors that were believed to have been dead, but that a new cable gave life to. He described huge factories, rolls of multicoloured wires, shipping containers filled to the brim, he narrated their journeys, the conditions of their goods. If a simple drop of sea water came into contact with a wire, it could change the destiny of the home in which it was fitted.

His voice had the tone of gusts of wind on the Atlantic, of waves rumbling onto the shore, of cicadas' wings rubbing against one another, the colour of wheat at the height of summer, the taste of blue crab from the Bering Sea.

When I left the shop, night had already fallen on Lyme Regis.

Face to face, we observe each other.

Babette's features are drawn. My nose is triple its normal size, the nasal wall is most definitely broken. My vision is slightly blurry, but it doesn't escape me that my partner doesn't seem to feel any pity for me. Rather, a little contempt. The house is silent, the kids in bed. We only hear a *drip-drip* when a drop of water falls in regular intervals from the tap. It's leaking. I should take care of it.

But for the moment, my universe is a mixture of the colours of lichen and the smell of peat, and on the tip of my tongue I have the taste of an exceptional black pepper. The ensemble is not at all a good omen. Neither for me, nor for Babette.

'We need to talk,' she eventually lets out, in one breath.

The time-honoured phrase for couples who swing between the last patch-up and the announcement of a storm that's even more destructive than the last.

We need to talk.

I almost hit her son. Is there anything more

unforgivable for a mother? No, probably not. She has been able to turn a blind eye to my artistic whims, my silences, my absences, my daydreams. She has been able to get used to living in the shadow of Liv and with the voice of Laïvely. She has been able to pretend to be happy in the Rabbit Hole and to accept that we now only rarely make love. She may even be able to imagine that she has reached some sort of contentment – that of the monotony that protects her from fate, from stormy weather. But forget that I physically attacked her son? What lie would she be able to tell herself in an attempt to justify what I did?

I put Laïvely in my office before we had dinner. She had remained silent, her green indicator fading in and out with the regularity of a well-behaved metronome. I watched her for a long time. Then I closed my eyes, searching through my memory for Liv's laugh, that laugh that had seduced me before I even discovered the face it belonged to. But it escaped me, and the more I forced myself to search for it, the more it concealed itself in the folds of my mind, where nonsensical images superimposed themselves; they pitched against one another, marching one after the other, accompanied by a howling soundtrack, unpleasant and evil. Had I been dreaming up Liv, and Laïvely was nothing but a reflection of my companion's imperfect soul? Or had I imagined things that didn't exist in order to fill the interior solitude in which I had been abandoned after the death of my lover?

I left Laïvely up in my office, alone and in the dark. I thought again, before closing the door on her, of David and his unique interpretation of home automation. I remembered his words and even the inflections of his voice. I could have transcribed it into music with a simple wave of my hand. All whilst Liv's laughter continued to escape me, as if I were no longer deserving of it. It was out of the question for me to rush to the shower to try and find it again. Besides, now I thought about it, I didn't remember hearing it for a while. Or it was just in that moment I was unable to bring to mind the times it had sung inside me – when it had truly resonated in the room, the result of a perfect harmony of flowing water and Laïvely's purring?

We need to talk.

Only my aunt's old-fashioned lampshade illuminates the room, diffusing a charmless, yellowish light that blurs the contours of the furniture. Babette's face stands out against the shadows. Old. Sad. Her eyes have lost their sparkle. Her lips are pursed, their usual vivid pink has turned sickly. The smell of peat intensifies. I don't feel like talking. I don't feel like arguing. What I did is inexcusable. I don't like Téo, but no one has asked me to like him. On the other hand, I am expected to control myself. Not to lift a hand to the child. Or any child. I am expected to behave like a responsible adult. A stepfather, what-ever that means. A man, if you will.

'I'm all ears.'

What else can I say? 'No, let's fuck and forget about it'? 'No, pack your bags and get out'? 'No, the sound of your voice reminds me of chalk scraping across a blackboard, I want to plug my ears, your colours are drab, ugly, off tonight and I only love you in Klein blue, with the scent of chlorine and the sound of throaty laughter'? The truth lies somewhere among all this. I'm just as eager to take my impulses further, to grab her without a hint of gentleness, to rip off her jeans and take her savagely on the table, where the remains of dinner have still not been cleared away, as I am to seize all her things with my hands and throw them out the window onto the street and let them sink into the muddy puddle that surrounds the lamp-post, the one that never seems to dry out. To let everything drown in the rain, in the grey, the black-and-white atmosphere of this spring in which the sun only shows itself sparingly, leaving us to our turmoil.

'What's got into you?'

London

Ellie has died. The funeral is packed. Cuddled up tightly next to me Liv holds back her tears with great difficulty. I composed the music for the ceremony, just like Ellie had asked me to in her last wishes. The piece, interpreted by a piano and a violin, is of great simplicity, almost a silence, or a nursling's breath. Despite that, the notes echo through the nave of the church as if ready to tear the roof off.

There were passages from the Bible, well-known and rehashed anecdotes, readings of affection and sadness. All of which left me with an image of immense solitude. After all, what did we know about our benefactress, beyond her conspicuous outfits, her taste for excess, her afternoon teas at The Ritz, the names of her dogs? Not a lot. Did she like sleeping alone, in the evening, in her huge bed, beneath a quilt that almost suffocated her? Would she have preferred to feel the animal warmth of a companion in misfortune? Incidentally, did she even like men? I had never seen her with anyone. In the end, everything that made her the person she was she had hidden from us.

We walked back home, our steps slow and heavy. We had to go and pick Lisa up from school, but even with that in mind, it wasn't enough to bring back our smiles.

The lawns of Hyde Park rolled insolently beneath the early springtime sun. Further along, down an alleyway, the horsemen trotted at a walking pace. An invisible dog yapped. Nannies pushed prams from which babbling sounds escaped. We didn't exchange a single word. Liv seemed to have switched off. She stumbled over a small stone and I caught her before she fell.

'Thanks,' she mumbled before continuing.

At Lancaster Gate, we crossed Bayswater Road to join Gloucester Terrace and headed towards Paddington Station. The noise was more intense, the traffic rushed by. Liv didn't seem to be taking in anything that surrounded us, and I led her like a guide dog leads its master. Within me rose chords, strange notes that summed up the story with our fairy godmother much better than those that had played out during the ceremony. Allegro. Yes, it was all allegro.

I smiled, and Liv threw an offended glance at me, as if a smile were an act of betrayal. I smiled a little more. I loved Liv's outbursts, her rages. On those rare occasions, her voice roared like a lake wounded by a speedboat cutting through it, taking on breadth, growing, growing, and crashing into me, a wave of wrath that nothing could stop. I never tried to provoke her fury, never, but when it erupted, I couldn't help but being charmed by it.

That day, Liv waited until we had closed the door of the house behind us before unleashing her anger. I got it all. I was heartless. I wasn't even human. I was incapable of the slightest emotion. What was wrong with me? What was that sketch of a smile that had floated across my lips throughout the whole ceremony? Indecent, shameful, pathetic – my behaviour drove her to dig out adjectives she rarely used, but which all tightened their grip around me, like blows from a paintbrush that precisely drew the portrait of a despicable man, worthy of the best of Dickens' novels.

I let her say everything she wanted to, knowing all too well the diverse forms that grief and mourning take on, knowing that she didn't know how else to express so much pain. She threw it up like others threw up hangovers, and I encouraged her to empty her heart, all the while with the same unbearable smile across my lips.

The crisis lasted a while. She struck at my torso

with her little fists before finally collapsing into my chest in tears, mumbling words of love as crazy and violent as the hateful ones she'd spat in my face moments before.

I took her to bed. I undressed her like one does a child, before making love to her like the woman she was. Her tears made way to little moans of pleasure, and she abandoned herself in one final cry.

When she fell asleep, I left to go and pick Lisa up from school. I thought I heard a cockerel. The sun had briefly disappeared behind a cloud black with darkness.

Upon our return, Piaf was singing of love throughout the whole house, and Liv, an apron tied around her waist, was making an apple pie.

We ended the day by painting strange shapes on big pieces of paper, each trying to get the other two to guess what we were attempting to represent. A silver christening cup served as a tumbler to wash our brushes. It told a story that was not ours, one of faith and belief, of blessings and confessions.

Liv smiled at me – her eyes had found their clear blue once more, a pure blue that allowed me to believe that I could read her soul. Now I smiled. I loved her and she was alive. Nothing else mattered.

Babette has fallen asleep, her warm body pressed against mine. She is one of the few people I know who sleeps stretched out on her back, arms flung over her head, abandoned and trusting in what the night has in store for her. Me, I fold in on myself to leave as little as possible to the spirits, the djinns, the monsters that lurk in the dark.

I listen to her even breathing, her steady breath. One, two, exhale; three, four, inhale. And it starts all over again.

We haven't spoken.

Earlier I had reached out to brush back a piece of her hair that was creeping onto her face. My fingers had strayed to her cheek, so round, so soft. Voluptuous. My thumb continued down to follow the contours of her mouth, from which a soft sigh escaped. Though words have often failed us, betrayed us, our bodies have always remained in harmony. The desire that I had buried beneath heavy silence was awakened with those simple caresses. I no longer wanted to rush into quick and diligent lovemaking, but to fill her slowly. To caress her breasts, her stomach, her back, her buttocks. To make my way down her body with my tongue, just until I reached that point, between her legs, that I already knew was coming to life for me. I wanted to go further, to massage her feet, to play with her toes. Then return slowly to the centre of her body and plunge in.

But I also knew that I couldn't expect her to accept my signs of tenderness – my thoughtless actions had prevented that. I continued to draw my fingers across her lips, patiently, hoping that she would suddenly find more desire to make love than war. Her eyelids lowered, she opened her lips slightly and the little tip of her tongue came to taste my finger.

In all relationships, there are those gestures, those words that seem trivial, that are nothing more than codes well known by the other, codes of permission. As Babette swallowed my thumb so as not to let it go, I knew I hadn't been forgiven – it would take a lot more for that – but I had been welcomed into a truce. A truce that both she and I wanted to be as gentle as possible.

We ended up on the kitchen tiles, beneath, rather than on the table, and as she straddled me, out-stretched on my sex, I watched her use me to take what she wanted, what she deserved. Then I understood that nothing was ever as simple, yet as complicated as an 'I love you' hurled at the other person when their body was joined to yours, when their sweat mixed with yours, when their pleasure took precedence over everything else...

Before this lullaby carries me away, I slowly get out of bed. The bedroom door spares me its usual creak as I close it behind me.

In my studio, Laïvely also seems to be asleep. Her conspicuous green is so pale that it seems white. I sit down on my piano stool and watch her. A metal tube. Electronic components. Wires of various colours. She is cold to the touch; I don't need to put my hand on her to know that. The mesh from which her voice escapes has aged slightly. It's tarnished, perhaps even threatening to rust in places. I watch her sleeping. Soothed, silent, calm. Mute.

The sensible thing to do would be to take her apart. To recycle each one of her components. To live in the present. To remove David's long speeches from my mind, a man distraught with loneliness in his shop where almost everything gathered dust, where the overly cluttered window display offered little interest to merry tourists, eager to buy a mug decorated with a dinosaur, a scene from *The French Lieutenant's Woman*, or an overexposed photo of the Cobb. I would be better off concentrating on Babette's laughter, which doesn't come often enough, rather than Liv's, which continues to escape me; and on fixing the cupboard doors, which now seem to have a life of their own.

I run my hand over my still-sore nose. How could this be anything other than a coincidence? Although my strange associations between taste, colour and noise, according to the day, play a greater or lesser role in my life, and although they have encouraged me not to be too rigidly Cartesian and have enabled me to accept that not everything in the universe can be explained rationally, they have never led me to the edge of madness – the real kind, the kind that drives you to take a forced chemical rest between four walls that are all but friendly, yet, in the state you find your-self in, become the height of comfort.

Laïvely is nothing more than a well-executed con-struction to which I dedicated months; a construction that fascinated me and seemed like the pinnacle of perfection because I found myself adding touches in-spired by Liv. I added a triangle, the sound of rain hitting a stream, a little transverse flute, a burst of clear harpsichord notes. But I don't remember in-corporating the more uncouth, brutal sounds, the cries and shrieks. David would explain to me that

these damn wires also make choices, that not everything depends on me. Maybe he's right, but how do I
know? By taking Laïvely apart, then putting her back
together, I'd have the beginnings of an answer. By
tightening the hinges on the cupboards, I'd stop them
hitting my face. A smile comes to play on my lips at
the thought of the garage door, resistant to any
change. If it were human, it'd probably be a grumbling, ageing male of one kind or another, clinging to
his convictions and certainties. But does that mean it
has a soul?

I hold out a hesitant hand. Then I pull it back.

Yes, I'd be better off responding to the commissions
that people still have the kindness to send me. If it
takes years to build up a reputation, it only takes a
few weeks to destroy it. They had pitied me at first,
in London. Then I was gradually forgotten. I only kept
in touch with Henry. In Paris, very few people knew
me. Not enough to notice my absences or my
presence. Soon, there won't be much left of my
savings.

I get up with a sigh. It's late, the moment in the
dead of night when you think the world has stopped
turning, that it's holding its breath. Laïvely still
doesn't react.

I leave the room without a last glance for her.

London

Henry has just left. He lives on the same mews; he moved here just a few days ago, and it seemed right to us, as neighbours, to invite him over for a drink. The evening went on a lot longer than we had imagined. Liv had already been in bed for a good while when Henry finally left, waving goodbye.

I close the door behind him, turn off the hallway light, leave the living room to its mess and go upstairs to join my wife and child.

Lying down against Liv's back, I smile. What a character! Only in London would you meet a guy like that.

Henry was born in Kenya during the time of British colonial rule. He had got to know the huge estates and the grand manor houses, the racecourses, the plethora of staff, the rainy season, the coffee plantations, Swahili.

After the country became independent in 1963, his parents wanted to return to the UK. He was ten years old at the time, and he has never really recovered from that first separation.

After studying anthropology, Henry roamed the

entire world, above all the roads less travelled. He discovered habits and customs that to him seemed easier to adapt to than those of 1980s England. Thatcher, punk and the royal family were stranger to him than certain rites of passage into adulthood practised by isolated African tribes.

Eventually, he stopped returning to his motherland, which, after all was simply adoptive. In the 1990s, he moved to Croatia. He remained silent about his reasons for his settling on the Dalmatian coast. It was for love, surely, I thought, without daring to ask the question. Then came the war, and the Adriatic paradise was tainted with blood. Henry, with a heavy heart, ended up back in the United Kingdom, and chose to hole up in the depths of Scotland. Despite finding it difficult to adapt to the environment, so different from the one he had grown used to, he quickly felt at home in those harsh, arid, uncompromising landscapes. He devoted himself to writing his books, to translating some of his texts into Swahili. He reread all the ancient Greek and Roman plays. He became interested in the history of the clans, tartan, and bagpipes. Above all, Rob Roy, discovered beneath the plume of Walter Scott, fascinated him. He wandered the lands of this Scottish Robin Hood, and in particular fell in love with Loch Katrine, whose shores the brigand was born on. Then the travel bug bit him again, snatching him from out of his books and carrying him away once more.

This time, it took him to the United States, where he went on tour to promote his latest book on the First Peoples. He particularly liked Maine and California, only had very few memories of Michigan, and did not feel what seemed like the obligatory infatuation for Montana, which left him unmoved. But Florida in particular captured his heart.

Henry found a miniscule island in the Keys and installed himself there until a raging hurricane passed through and forced him to continue on his way.

It was our mews where he had come to find refuge.

Henry liked music. In fact, he knew of some of my compositions. But what pleased him most of all was when music, rightly so, was born out of somewhere least expected.

'In Florida, when I went to Marathon to restock once a week,' he told me, 'I would always stop at the same tiki bar. It wasn't much to look at – it was on the side of the US1 highway. It was a little grungy, a little old fashioned, full of rough-looking types in sleeveless leather jackets, who were probably busy smuggling everything they could out of Cuba. They didn't like Latinos, despised them even – you could tell. Real white trash. However, in this bar, there was Pedro. He came from Peru, and not Cuba, but for all the others, it was *tomayto tomhato*. Pedro made the best coffee I had ever drunk. One day, we got talking, he and I. And the next time he invited me to his place. And there, he got out an instrument that I'd never seen before: a donkey's jawbone.'

Henry laughed upon seeing my reaction.

'Yes, Stan, a donkey's jawbone! Complete with all its teeth. And Pedro started to play it. I'd never heard anything so strange,' he concluded, getting lost in his memories.

I let him daydream for a moment before bringing him back.

'But how is it played?'

'Oh, it's quite simple. You just tap the jawbone and the teeth rattle like little ossicles. The music comes from their enamel hitting the bone. I assure you, the melody is surprisingly sweet. I think it's called a *kijada*, or a *quijada*. A percussion instrument, actually. Primitive and elaborate at the same time. You can also run a stick along the teeth, but my, that sound got on my nerves – it was a bit like scratching a chalkboard, you see. Anyway, there were many ways to use that jawbone to make music, believe me.'

I remained silent. I wondered what the notes carried

by teeth would sound like. Notes made of bone. And from a donkey, whose braying was one of the most detestable noises I'd ever heard. And I spoke as a connoisseur. After all, I had grown up on a farm, hadn't I?

There are silences that are more booming than symphonies. The one that had fallen onto the Rabbit Hole was of that scale and started, insidiously, to suffocate all efforts at life, at laughter, at joy. It suffocated the furniture, the walls, the windows, it deprived us of air, of the breath that was necessary for confrontation, war, and, de facto, peace.

The days pass. I get the feeling that I am part of an awful play, an adaptation of a work straight out of the *nouveau roman* movement, where the words kill all desire to turn the page to discover the next. I repeat the same movements and gestures, morning and evening. I say the same 'good mornings' and the same 'have a good days'. The same 'all goods' and the same 'dinner's readys'. Babette peels the carrots and grates them. I run away from the sound for the necessary time. We eat in silence. Téo's mop grows longer over his forehead and shaved sides. Laïvely doesn't utter a word.

Our bed is cold, frozen. It's as if Babette is finding it even more difficult to forgive herself for having given into her desire than me for my outburst of violence. She hasn't brought up that evening again. If Téo explained to her the reason I'd lifted a hand to him, she has kept that information to herself. Her behaviour could even be described as passive-aggressive. But in reality, it's just a reflection of the daze she's in: how did she get here? She can't answer that question any more than I can.

During the day I remain bound to my piano, whose keys I no longer dare to even brush. My memories are becoming entangled. Henry. David. Coloured wires and mouths that snigger to reveal teeth that time and neglect have yellowed. The pink of that London house drips, and bloody streams furrow through its foundations. I have the taste of paprika in my mouth, a taste that nothing can get rid of.

Sometimes a step creaks without reason, and I think I hear the squeak of the garage door. When, rarely, I go out into the little yard and gaze up at the house, I have the impression that the rabbit has moved, that he's got closer to Alice and is ready to take her by the hand and lead her down an endless hole, right to the heart of the world.

My nose changes colour, and only its variations mark the passage of time. I am vaguely aware that the holidays are approaching. But Babette doesn't bring Landes up again – camping, surfing, the whisper of the waves and the laughter of the sea. Day after day we bury a body whose identity I do not know. Us? Our relationship? Our love? Our future? Our dreams? The tomb digs and digs itself deeper and deeper, just like the puddle under the lamppost gets bigger and bigger, to the point where it is sometimes difficult to guess if it's daybreak or the end of the day.

David and his wires. Henry and his donkey's jawbone.

My nights are populated with strange dreams that give me no respite. I don't remember ever being so tired. Even after Liv's death the world held on to some colours. Light scents too. Now, there's nothing left. A spidery veil settles on every surface it can cling to. It will surely end up suffocating us one day.

I can't see a way out of this situation. Making a decision about anything is far beyond me. I should, at the very least, apologise. Yet I am incapable of doing so; a strange torpor has taken hold of me. I'm living, moving and breathing in slow motion.

Yesterday the telephone rang, and I couldn't pick it up. Whoever it was called again. My action, once again, remained unfinished. After two more attempts, they gave up. Like I have given up, once again, a part of what I was, stripping myself of another part of my humanity.

I don't recognise my reflection in the lacquer of the piano.

I really am exhausted.

London

Henry became a regular in the pink house. He would knock briefly in the evening before letting himself in – we'd rarely lock the front door before we went to bed. He would join us for dinner, and he would tell an amazed Lisa stories that were brimming with the scent of strange undergrowth and even stranger sounds. Very quickly she abandoned her Beatrix Potter books in favour of Henry's knees and his memories, which seemed far crazier than anything that could happen to a family of rabbits who drank their tea from porcelain cups and whose mother wore an apron tied around her waist. As the months went by, she also began to snub Piglet, despite having given him the title of best friend. Now, all she dreamt of were wildebeest and giraffes, bows and arrows, and she begged us to let her fetch water from the well before the lions sur-rounded the nearest watering hole. At school, things got complicated – her little classmates didn't believe a word she said. But instead of letting it go, Lisa con-fronted them, and didn't hesitate to kick and slap when words were no longer enough.

We were called in by an exasperated schoolteacher. Henry agreed to go into the school to speak a little about his experiences in front of the class, in order to prove that Lisa was not spinning tales. She had her moment of glory. The requests to come and play at the house after school streamed in. A parade of more or less well-behaved little girls marched through our door. Liv baked cakes and biscuits for them in the morning before going to work. It was left to me to take care of the little ladies and watch over them as, in threes of fours, their over-excited laughter invaded the house after school. I played the piano for them, sang, we invented nursery rhymes together. Henry was not always present. This wild admiration, he apologised with a contrite smile, was making him dizzy. I understood. He, the old lone wolf with a thousand lives, was growing tired of this demanding, talkative and feminine audience.

Sometimes he disappeared for a few days, but we never worried. He would always end up sneaking back into the living room, more often at brandy time than teatime, and we would continue our conversations from where we left off, as if they had never been interrupted.

We missed Ellie. Often, at the weekend, we'd go for a stroll in Kensington for the simple pleasure of walking in front of her house. The place that had been so warm and welcoming, where we had spent such beautiful moments, was already withering away without its mistress. The weeds had started to overrun the front garden. The windows were tarnished, under attack from rain and pollution. The house seemed to be shrinking in on itself, locked up in its silence, its abandoned rooms closed off. We didn't know if Ellie had heirs, nor what would become of the place. Once our friend had disappeared, the relationships we'd forged through her had unravelled by themselves, and faster than we could have imagined. We had been naïve. What did we have in common with a lord and former ambassador to Kinshasa, a multi-award-winning actress or an archbishop? Nothing, except Ellie.

Liv refused to visit her grave. She didn't like cemeteries. They scared her. Reading *The Canterville Ghost* at the age of ten had really marked her, and nothing scared her more than the idea of finding herself in the shoes of the twins' sister, obliged to help a desperate ghost find peace of mind. These superstitions she sometimes admitted to only made her even dearer to me.

After a while, we stopped walking past Ellie's house. It depressed us too much.

We had known Henry for almost a year when one evening he turned up with a smile like a Cheshire cat, an unusually shaped package tucked under his arm. Lisa jumped up, tried to hang off his neck and grab the package from him. But Henry, whilst willing to play along, wouldn't let her win.

'My little dear, patience is the mother of all virtues,' he declared as he lifted whatever was wrapped in newspaper above his head, out of Lisa's reach.

She finally grew bored, but to show her displeasure, she went up to her bedroom, stamping her feet with each step, surly.

Henry chuckled – he couldn't be fooled. And he wouldn't bend so quickly. It wouldn't be long before she'd once again find her place atop his knees.

'So, Stan, how's it going?'

'Good, the teas with the little ladies have started to slow down a bit and I'm working again.'

He giggled and placed the mysterious package in the pram that had slowly become part of the furniture – no one had found the need or the time to assign it a new home once Lisa no longer had a need for it.

I served him a brandy just as he liked it, got out a packet of dry biscuits that I laid out on a blue plate and joined him in the living room.

I noticed that Henry seemed to have aged since his

last visit, only a few weeks earlier. Suddenly, I realised that he was an elderly man. Just like Ellie, he wasn't eternal, and one day he too would have to leave us.

In the light that fell over London that mid-afternoon, I had the vision of losses to come, of those that awaited us, and my heart clenched.

Liv and I were not, for a whole host of reasons, close to our families. We were content with the happiness that came with one another's company, with our life as a threesome. Sometimes, someone found their place with us, like Ellie in her time, like Henry later. Only Laila could be considered a friend, but even with her, our links were stretched thin. We'd gone back to see her in Dorset a couple more times, but our lives had become so different that we didn't have a lot to say to each other, and Liv wasn't the type to maintain long-distance friendships. Or family relationships for that matter. I'd only seen her parents a few times, and her sister even fewer. It wasn't that Liv had cut ties with them, more that she had built a life in which they didn't really have a place, as if their roles had ended when she had flown the nest.

From my side, my 'idiosyncrasies' had made me a loner from a young age. Sure, my brothers and sisters had always accepted me for who I was, without caring about my differences, but despite that, we had grown distant in adulthood. We had become strangers connected only by blood.

Watching my daughter grow and play at tea parties with her little friends, chatting with my wife about piano chords, a Verdi opera, the perfect shade of make-up, I was fulfilled. I didn't need anything more.

And it was probably because Henry never asked us for anything, and also didn't need us, that we got along so well. We owed each other nothing.

He finished his brandy, placed his glass on the pallet that served as our coffee table and struggled to his feet. When he reached the pram, he took out the package and unwrapped the newspaper surrounding it. A donkey's jawbone appeared. An impressive jawbone, with teeth that seemed to smile with a demonic grin.

I left the house today. I had got it into my head to find
a donkey's jawbone somewhere in Paris so I could
play it again. Yesterday I spent the day watching
videos on YouTube in which the instrument reigned.
I associated its acoustics with rhubarb and a strange
mosaic of cement tiles, like the ones found in
Provencal homes. I found myself hypnotised by the
wobbly teeth, by the play of hands on the concave
bone. And little by little, I became possessed by the
idea of having this strange instrument in my hands
once more.

I walked along the street, to a different beat than
those around me. They walked quickly, advanced in
a straight line, shoulders tucked in, chin to neck, eyes
to the ground, avoiding all other gazes, trying to
weave through the raindrops of yet another down-
pour. And then there was me, head high, smile on my
lips, I seemed to be dancing across the grey pavement
in which my body was reflected, distorted by the
puddles. A funny sort of music filled my skull. A kind
of symphony in which the diverse cries of animals

from the savannah took precedence over string instruments. It was like an inverted *Peter and the Wolf*, or rather the very opposite of the famous musical tale. I skipped along in time to hyenas' cries and elephants' trumpets, carried by images and smells that belonged only to me, for this savannah smelt strangely of roses and shallots.

I was so caught up in this internal spectacle that I ended up losing my way. I had intended to go to the Gare Saint-Lazare district, where there were plenty of musicians' dens to be found, but when I finally opened my eyes to what was actually around me, I ended up finding myself in Place de Vosges. The chances of coming across the instrument that I had decided to get my hands on, whatever the cost, were slim.

Suddenly exhausted, I collapsed onto a bench. It was damp and it wasn't long before my trousers were soaked through. Everything smelt of petrol, dog shit and wet sand. I was ready to cry.

An old lady who walked past, dragging her shopping trolley behind her – a survivor of the gentrification of the neighbourhood – mistook my appearance and discreetly slipped a coin into my cold hand, offering me a smile. I automatically responded with a foggy smile of my own and a shaky 'thank you' without really understanding her gesture. I was happy to accept it, for what else could I have done? I hadn't just lost my way, I had lost myself along the way. I had no idea who I was or where I was going. What was I doing there? I didn't even recognise the city that surrounded me, it was foreign to my body, just as my body was to me.

Nothing made sense, I could no longer remember why I had left the house. I got to my feet, clutching the fairy godmother's coin tightly in my fingers. What use could it be to me?

Sinking my hand into the pocket of my raincoat, I found something cold. It was cylindric, metallic. In the light of day, I seemed to recognise it. I blinked slowly several times, at the same speed as the green dot that flashed on and off at a slow and regular rhythm on one of its sides. Tears traversed my face as the savannah fell silent. Only the pure sound of the triangle could be heard.

Sure, it would be crazy to say that Laïvely brought me back home. But I couldn't otherwise explain how I managed to get back. Nor why I even went to the effort of doing so. Because my feeling of foreignness, of being distant, my incomprehension of the world around me, persisted.

Before crossing the threshold I studied Alice and the rabbit for a long time, all whilst playing the garage door, that behaving as it should, whistled its own melody. I thought I remembered that Alice had trouble getting out of the rabbit hole, that she was growing, or it was shrinking, but I'm not sure anymore. But I do remember that she had feared suffocating there, that she was judged by the cards, the loopy king and queen. I think there was also something about a trial. Was Alice scared, or did she scare them?

I hesitated to enter the Rabbit Hole, the idea of being devoured by the place tempting me only weakly. Then I shrugged. After all, what else was there to do? Laïvely hummed 'Que sera, sera', and I finally pushed open the door to the house.

When she got back, Babette found me planted like a stake in the entrance. I was staring at my reflection in the mirror opposite me. Laïvely was in my hand, and I was clutching her as if my life depended on her. She seemed to be whining and whimpering gently; my raincoat was still soaked, dripping. Babette called out my name several times before managing to shake me out of my cathartic state. She was scared because I didn't seem to recognise her, she told me later, even once she had washed me and put me to bed.

Babette had taken matters, or rather me, into her own hands. She managed to get me upstairs and into a hot bath and get me to drink a hot cup of tea while I nervously chattered my teeth. Like calming an edgy horse, she stroked my arm, my neck, my hair, all whilst talking to me in a low voice, telling me I don't know what – it all went in one ear and out the other just as quickly. But the melody of her voice was enough. Little by little, I came back, regained my body and my present. My past too. My past above all, under the watchful eye of Laïvely on the sink.

I'm in bed now and from the ground floor the hubbub of an ordinary evening rises. Babette's voice, the voice of her son, deeper as he is coming to the end of puberty. Lisa is silent, or she can't manage to make herself heard all the way up the stairs. Crockery clatters, a glass hits the sink. A carafe slides across the waxed tablecloth, a chair scrapes. They're having dinner.

My crisis – how else can I describe my afternoon absence? – had the positive effect of breaking the cloak of silence that Babette and I were drowning in, dragging our offspring with us. Confronted by my still-bruised face, my haggard expression, my partner had behaved like a mother, a loving and devoted wife.

She had cared for me, comforted me, given me all the tenderness she could muster. She had shown gentleness, compassion and kindness.

We will speak no more of my violence, of my screaming at her son. We will speak no more of our disagreements, of our inconsistencies. I know we won't. We will pretend that everything has been resolved, when nothing has been. And one day, that false note will sound out in a well-oiled composition, shattering the newfound harmony. Like the crash of a symbol that comes too soon and destabilises the whole orchestra. Like a pinch of cinnamon in an apple pie, with which the cook has been too heavy handed.

Our relationship is cracking, and these small fissures threaten to become the rifts that will engulf us.

On my bedside table, Laïvely flickers softly. I seem to hear her humming a nursery rhyme, one Liv used to sing to Lisa to console her when she was overcome with sadness, to open the door to her dreams. But I'm wary of my senses, no longer sure if something is the fruit of my memory or the observation of my surroundings.

The scent of lemon verbena tickles my nostrils. A cherry kiss seems to land on my lips.

London

Lisa was scared of the jawbone, so Henry had to take it back, to my great despair. I was sure I would have been able to use it for crazy, unique, never-heard-before compositions. But Lisa was more important than anything else, and it was out of the question to make her believe that the thing had left the house only for her to then find it stashed away somewhere.

Liv had put weight on, which suited her well. She had traded in her seventies-style clothes, her long skirts and colourful gilets, for a sager style: black trousers – velour in winter, cotton in summer; white shirts – long or short sleeved according to the season; and Repetto ballerina flats. Her hair too had now been tamed, Aunt Agathe's barrette holding it calmly in place.

She had got a promotion and was managing an entire troupe of young make-up artists and costume designers, now rarely putting her own hand to the palette. She had discovered a new passion for infusions and drank mint-verbena, liquorice and thyme, and other, spicier blends that filled the house with their fragrances upon her return.

I thought she was beautiful. She was always so beautiful. And desirable. Despite everything, our relationship, which we had believed immune to the passing of time, no longer had anything of the excitement that had underpinned it for so many years. Liv sometimes got carried away, losing her patience over trivial things. Silly little issues – a badly rinsed teapot or the corner of a page folded down in a book. Her tone became more grating. She would utter sharp, guttural phrases, let out a groan, then leave the room, to come back a few minutes later, smiling, a caress at the tips of her fingers. I didn't pay too much attention to her mood swings. I knew they were short-lived and that I was unable to understand at the time that the teapot, that the book, hid a bigger dissatisfaction, one that she was incapable of expressing.

Liv made a new friend, Ranya, with whom she regularly went out and who met her one evening a week to go to a yoga class. I often saw Henry, spent hours on the phone to David, who continued to repair absolutely anything, and I had even started to frequent the British Library, where I haphazardly took out books for the simple pleasure of spending hours in one of the large study rooms, watching the other readers and analysing the ballet of the archivists. Often, I'd treat myself to lunch in the cafeteria, and if it was too crowded, I'd find myself sharing my table with students, professors, enthusiasts of Henry VIII or Mary Stuart, contemporary art, or ancient Rome. Sometimes we talked. Sometimes I listened to them talk.

There were people of all ages, of all walks of life, some had even crossed the Channel for two or three days to work on the documents available in the reading room.

One day, I got talking to Ryan, who was passionate about the cuisine in the court of Elizabeth I. The next week, I learned almost everything from Mary's mouth about the benefits of lavender. There were also Jack, Maddie, France, Thomas, John, Lisbette and many others who enlightened me on quantum physics, melting permafrost, black holes, poetry from the time of Shakespeare and countless other subjects I remember nothing about.

Those encounters, furtive, and which never gave rise to long-term friendships, nor even short-lived ones, allowed me to make Liv believe that I too was no longer alone. Or more so, that I too was expanding the bubble in which the two of us, then the three of us, had wallowed, and that I was taking pleasure in doing so.

I felt that Liv was reassured by my gossip from the

reading room, as if it were essential that we should each follow our own path, paths I was convinced would only serve to distance us from one another, just as I was convinced that there was no point at all in pointing this out to her.

I played the game. For love, at first, then out of real curiosity. I never would have believed that my contemporaries could be so interested in such a wide range of subjects, to the point of devoting entire days, and in even, in some cases, entire lives to them. I was fascinated above all by the blend of scents and colours that their words unearthed in me, sensations that I tried, with varying degrees of success, to transcribe onto my piano each evening. I discovered the power of hyacinths and lilies when their perfumes collided with that of Canadian apples covered in brown sugar and baked in the oven. I savoured the petroleum blue associated with the sound of the djembe. I let myself go, swept away by the scent of orange blossom that mixed with the taste of a lamb tagine garnished with prunes and almonds.

From all of this emerged a strange, gentle symphony, punctuated by more violent drumbeats. And it was an astonishing success.

I start to recognise myself in mirrors again whenever I cross paths with them. The swelling in my nose has gone down, and just one black eye is there to remind me of the cupboard incident. At home, for about ten days now, the atmosphere has been calmer, pacified. I don't know if we're in the eye of the storm, experiencing the last bit of peace before the elements unleash themselves again, or if the tempest is well and truly behind us. And I don't try to find out the answer. I take advantage of this period to go out a little more, looking for, maybe unconsciously, the inspiration that has been running away from me for too long.

The weather has also changed, in tune with life in the Rabbit Hole. The sun is more candid, more cheerful. The buds are blooming. The plane trees, from one day to the next, are bursting with brilliant green leaves. It's like suddenly being in a musical from the 1960s; sooner or later I expect to see Fred Astaire rehearsing a tap number under the lamppost at the end of the street.

Laïvely seems to be in harmony with all this. She is normal again, at least I can no longer detect the slightest hint of strangeness in her. She answers my questions, plays Satie when I'm reading, informs me of the temperature when I'm about to leave the house, reminds me to take my paracetamol at the given hour. Her voice does not contain the slightest trace of emotion, her lights are green. I've almost come to believe that in the last few weeks I've been dreaming up her nastiness, her perversity.

Téo continues to eat like a pig and wash as little as possible; Lisa remains herself, smiling, silent and gentle. In the evenings, before going to sleep, she caresses the quilt her mother made for her with her thumb. I went back to Buttes-Chaumont with her yesterday – it smelt of candy floss and waffles, there were children screaming as they rode past on their bikes, mothers smiling as they watched their youngest play in the sandpit. The atmosphere was spring-like, bucolic, serene. A postcard Paris. We ate a sugar-lemon crepe, drank a lemonade, and as we walked home hand in hand, Lisa thanked me with a smile that was studded with little white sparkles that looked like snowflakes.

This morning, in my studio, I listened to my *Symphony BL,* the one I wrote after my weeks spent at the British Library. I found some faults in the composition, but nothing too bad. What was more disturbing was that it didn't evoke any emotion in me. Nothing. Neither scents nor colours, everything around me remained a neutral dove grey. I deduced that I hadn't quite been cured yet. That perhaps I needed to actually start working, rather than just waiting to be inspired, which is all I had been doing until now.

So, I've been practising scales for two hours. The notes rise to the rhythm of my fingers on the keys. But all I hear is the silence that surrounds them. Technically, I've lost nothing, the movement is still there, full, poised, lively when it needs to be. But everything else has disappeared.

There's a light knock at my door.

'Stan?'

I freeze. Red invades my field of vision. A blood red. A red synonymous with violence, with killing, with pain and agony.

Another knock.

'Stan?' Babette insists.

Doesn't she understand that it's forbidden to interrupt me when I'm playing? Doesn't she know?

I ignore her and continue to pummel out the notes through the veil of blood that hides the piece, the piano, life from my eyes.

The distinctive sound of the handle twisting scrapes my ear drums. I press harder on the keys, accelerate my playing. I never take the risk, I always lock it. I whisper to Laïvely to play *Aïda*, the march of the trumpets. The music rises in an interpretation performed at La Scala in Milan. One of my favourites. I was there. The beginning of the 2000s. A sumptuous performance, the height of opera itself. Liv was enthralled at my side, taking her hand away from mine to press it against her thrilled heart. The vein in her neck pulsed. Tears of emotion filled her eyes with pearls.

The Chorus of the Hebrew Slaves from *Nabucco* would surely have been a wiser choice, and Laïvely seems to think so too, because here comes the song of the slaves crying for their lost homeland. And my tears flow to the rhythm of their lament, drowning everything but my own pain.

I no longer hear Babette's voice, nor the squeaking handle. I hear nothing but the opera that sounds out, the suffering of the choir that echoes mine. A vague scent of warm earth, almost burnt by the sun, rises to my nostrils as my studio drapes itself in colours of fire.

And I close my eyes, safe and devastated at the same time.

London

Success is a strange thing. Thank God that that of composers remains more private than that of a film star. I wasn't recognised in the street, but on the other hand, the phone was ringing off the hook: journalists from the specialist press, directors of operas small and large, other composers, men of theatre, music, letters, women too.

Liv was beside herself. We went out together more often, and she saw Ranya less. We re-established connections with the world we knew thanks to Ellie, but this time we entered it through the front door. Some of the people who were now inviting me to dinner didn't recognise me as the young guy who, just a few years earlier, brought their piano to life during their society cocktail hours. They'd even forgotten our names. Liv and I laughed at these slightly ridiculous situations, such as the time I had to kiss the hand of a lady covered in jewels, whose wrinkles looked like they were lacquered onto her face, they moved so little. She wore the appropriate smile on her lips, this lady who had forgotten that this same hand had once discreetly slipped me an envelope stuffed with notes to pay for the performance I had given.

Wherever she was, Ellie was surely doubled over with laughter at seeing us like that. She would have loved this new twist of fate. And she would surely have given herself credit for it, with the characteristic bad faith of those who, in order to live, need to be the shining light at the centre of their circle.

We went out often in those days. We found ourselves once again in the salons of Chelsea and Kensington, in beautiful, lavish dwellings, or large modern apartments with breath-taking views of the Thames. I was asked about my projects. People were rarely interested in Liv's work, despite the fact she was by no means a stranger to the game. But some habits die hard, and the only woman who in those circles had the right to shine so brightly she eclipsed the power of the men present was Her Majesty herself.

We usually went home late. Often on foot, finding the same pleasure we had for these strolls in the first moments of our love. Liv had conserved her light ballerina steps, despite not being as slight as she had been previously. I imitated her rhythm, my arm through hers. We crossed Hyde Park to join Bayswater Road, then on to our neighbourhood of Paddington.

The park was calm – I loved it at any hour of the day or night. Just as I loved to see Liv imitate a guest who lacked finesse in his analysis of the music, or the accent of another so snobbish he was almost a caricature, or the way a trophy wife fluttered her eyelashes, because in that milieu – like so many others that were less aristocratic but where money flowed freely – there was no escaping the circus of odd characters. Sometimes, on the way home, she would hum a Piaf song – she was my wife's favourite singer at the time. We even, one drunken evening, had the idea of dancing in a dark back alley, Liv in her black trousers, a reddish lock of hair caressing her face, and me, my eternal scarf around my neck, embracing her, holding her tightly against me, knowing that I was living one of those moments of joy that have the power to make us suffer for their absence, whilst in the very moment, their fullness delights our hearts.

Most often, Henry was our babysitter. Lisa's affection for him never wavered. She had forgiven him for the donkey's jawbone, just as she had forgiven him for toasting bread too much and unevenly spreading the butter and jam she was partial to. Upon our return, she would already be sleeping, Henry snoring too on the old sofa, a book open on his knees.

He took them from our shelves. He said that the books in a house could tell its inhabitants' secrets. They harboured their dreams, their dashed hopes, their journeys and their loves. What did he learn about us leafing through Maupassant, Dostoyevsky, Malraux, Pasternak, Iris Murdoch, Agatha Christie or even Nick Hornby? Had he discovered, hidden behind our Limoges porcelain plates, our stash of American detective novels? Did he prefer the tales and legends that adorned Lisa's bedroom corner? He never gave anything away. But at some of his remarks, I realised just how right he was. Our books really spoke to who we were, our temperaments, the story of our love at first sight.

Liv would greet him with a kiss on the cheek, patting him on the arms before going up to bed, leaving us alone. We'd serve ourselves a drink, a glass of brandy for him, gin or rum for me, and the evening would continue with pointless discussions, the kind which go by almost without words, both of us so tired our heads spun, the night already well under way.

It wasn't unusual for Henry to leave in the early hours of the morning. I would then be left alone in the living room, trying to catch a glimpse of the timid sun rising over the city. I listened to the silence filled with the presence of my wife and my daughter, sometimes having the impression that their breath reached me from the bedroom. During those blessed hours, when in a flash one can measure the weight of one's happiness, it is so tangible, I was absolutely alive. Everything was in its place. Colours, scents and sounds were in harmony. And new compositions were taking shape in me.

All that remained to do was lay them to sleep on a stave, like tucking in a well-behaved child. It was all so easy.

At the table Babette acts as if nothing is wrong.

'Can you pass the salt please?'

'Sure.'

Téo avoids my gaze, his nose in his noodles. Babette has cooked-up a stir-fry with crunchy vegetables.

'It's delicious.'

'Thanks.'

It's true, it is delicious. The touch of sesame breaks the ensemble a little – I've never really been fond of the taste or consistency of the little seeds – but it doesn't matter.

'By the way, I knocked on your door earlier, but I don't think you heard me.'

'Ah, really? Sorry, I didn't.'

'The campsite called. They had a last-minute cancellation. A bungalow's free. I told them we'd take it.'

'Uh huh.'

I chew the stubborn broccoli. Nausea comes over me.

'In fact,' she explains, occupied with piling green

peppers and courgettes onto her fork, 'the bungalow is one of the smallest. As you didn't really seem to be too thrilled about the idea of a holiday, I'll go alone with Téo.'

She finishes speaking and lifts her head, waiting for my response. In her eyes I note an air of defiance that contends with a certain sadness. I don't want to know which will win.

'I'm sorry, but you didn't answer. They were waiting on the phone so I had to make a decision.'

I try a smile. I'm sure too many of my teeth are on show. I'm grinning. A donkey's jawbone frozen in a silent bray.

'You did the right thing, of course. It's a good idea.'

Téo's chair scrapes the floor. He leaves the kitchen mumbling a vague, 'I've got homework.'

Lisa stays in her seat, silent as always. But I have an uneasy feeling. She is sensitive to the slightest change in atmosphere. Despite this, I avoid putting my hand on her shoulder to reassure her. I know this gesture would be misinterpreted by Babette because she needs my undivided attention, she needs me to remain focused on the messages she is sending me via her words, her eyes, and the slightest of her silences. Words become dangerous traps, landmines with the power to kill. Silence is no better.

Babette's shoulders seem to sink slightly. Disappointment or relief? I don't want to know the answer, not now, not just yet. I know, however, that I will not get away with it as easily as this. It has all gone away too smoothly. There are some things that a mother just cannot let go. We've experienced ten or so days of favourable winds, but the decision that Babette has just made, and which I am not against, has unlocked a floodgate that, if opened, has deadly potential. Did she, on a whim, out of provocation, say yes to the campsite, knowing full well that I was behind my door and had simply chosen to ignore her? Does her anger with me have deeper roots, which my every move nourishes? Or is it simply that she can breathe easier knowing she'll spend her holiday alone with her son? They have their own codes, their own memories, their own way of being together, and, after all, Lisa and I are as much a disruptive element in their equation as their being in the Rabbit Hole.

I take another bite even though I'm no longer hungry. At least there's no chance of someone asking me to talk when I have my mouth full. Of course, I'm not going to be able to spend the days until they leave with my mouth constantly stuffed with food, but for the moment, I see no way to put an end to the discussion. Babette is not fooled. She gives me a weak smile as she clears her plate. Lisa takes hers to the sink.

They both leave the room, leaving me alone with my mountain of broccoli. Could I make it last until tomorrow?

I've come to smoke a cigarette in the garage. Lisa has gone to bed. Babette is in front of the television watching a nondescript Netflix series. I'm pretending to be looking for a screwdriver. I don't think she really cares what I'm up to.

I've slipped Laïvely into the pocket of my dressing gown. She softly plays an extract from *My Fair Lady*. I hum along. I think of nothing as I take a drag of my cigarette.

Its glowing tip hypnotises me. It blazes and sizzles. I love the sound, the glow, more than the taste of the tobacco on my tongue. I should try to write it, give it notes, another consistency, a sweeter flavour. Yes, I should.

London

It was during that technicolour period in which joy spoke for itself that I learned of Aunt Agathe's death and her legacy. For a while, we had thought of using it as an opportunity to visit Paris and France as a family, Lisa having never set foot in the country, but we quickly gave up on the idea. Liv had too much work, and the school holidays weren't due for a while yet.

So, I left for Paris alone, a quick return visit to put all the formalities related to the house in order.

I had never really liked the city where I'd only ever come for medical appointments, to meet doctors and visit their surgeries, and more often than not inhospitable paediatric wards. The solicitor's office was near Place de l'Odéon. Once the papers had been signed, I took myself on a walk through the Jardin de Luxembourg, watched some boats bobbing in the pools and observed the plump pigeons waddling along the pathways before leaving the park through the gate leading out onto Saint-Germain-des-Prés and being swallowed up by the metro to get to the house.

Standing in front of the gate, I was assailed by a strange sense of familiarity. I could almost feel my mother's hand holding mine, and her perfume came back to me. Of Aunt Agathe remained the memory of a generous woman who smelt just like freshly baked cakes, and whose pearly laughter bounced off the walls of the living room. In my childhood eyes, she was an old lady, but she must have only been in her mid-forties when we last saw her. She had always been gentle and attentive towards me, whilst never really showing any curiosity about the child I really was, that silent child whose interior world was populated by scents, colours, and sounds, all so specific. I still wonder what she had seen in me, to have given me, years later, this house, and with it a part of her life.

I entered a shadowy and dusty hallway. The house seemed to sigh, already tired at the thought of my intrusion. It was on tiptoes, as if concerned with disturbing it as little as possible, that I surveyed the rooms of the ground floor, looking for a clue that would explain this inheritance, a trace of Agathe and her daughter, still wondering what my aunt had wanted to offer me beyond those walls and those floors.

I believed I'd found the answer when I opened the

door into the garage and it emitted the sound that belonged only to it, the sound that had delighted me so much as a child. I played it for a moment, my eyes closed, rediscovering the taste of mussels and fries, churros and chocolate and green tea that the sound had always brought to mind for me. In that moment, I stopped being a man, instead becoming the little boy from back then, dazzled by those notes that no instrument could ever reproduce. Had Agathe understood before everyone else that music would be my redemption and my salvation? Was it these notes that she had left me? These notes, or their potential? Was that the key to the Rabbit Hole, the path I had to take to find a universe more my size? The mystery remains. As for the paths offered by music, I had been walking them for more than two decades now, and they had finally delivered me from the strange child I had been.

In her bedroom, on the dressing table, the pink rococo barrette caught my attention. I don't remember ever having seen her wear it. I picked it up, turned it over in my fingers, before stuffing it into my pocket. It would be a present for Liv, it would harmonise perfectly with the red of her hair.

My cousin's bedroom had not changed since my last visit. Frozen in time, a mausoleum dedicated to a life cut short, it still smelt of the Cacharel that Elisabeth loved to spritz herself with before slipping into her dance shoes and offering me a demonstration of her talent. Those pointe shoes still lay just alongside her neatly made bed, as if she had just slipped them off. On the wall were posters of David Hamilton, quotes from Baudelaire, photos of holidays, an adolescent girl's entire world laid bare, her secrets, her hopes, and her dreams. On the bed was an old, well-loved doll, her hair sparse, her dress full of holes, her hand-knitted jumper frayed by time. I left the room overwhelmed by sadness and gave up on any further inspection.

On the Eurostar that evening, on the way back to London, I played with the barrette for a moment. Then the joy of heading home took over all the feelings that had been with me for the whole day. As the miles went by, I put my childhood, France and my family back into a corner of my heart and my memory, not wishing to dwell on them any longer. It was not that I had been unhappy during those years – far from it. Life on the farm had been simple and full of love. But the Stan of that time was no longer, and had not been for a long time. And if the new Stan crossed paths with him, I'm not sure he would have liked him. His strangeness had become strange to me. I had rebuilt myself differently, not on the foundations laid during my youth, but on those that I had established upon my arrival in London. What I was then was not an extension of what I once had been. No. I had nothing in common with that Stan, and that's what that trip to Paris had taught me. Agathe had been mistaken, I had not grown up by taming and mastering my differences. I had become my differences. And a happy man. As happy as anyone could be.

I haven't seen a soul this morning. I pretended to be sleeping – I could no longer stuff my face in order to avoid conversation. Of course, I've missed Lisa, but I'll make up for it tonight.

When I finally head downstairs, the house is silent, apart from Laïvely's soft humming. Yes, she hums at very specific moments when she feels content. It's rare. Besides, maybe I only hear her hum when the silence surrounding her is of an extreme quality: if it were a painting it would be polar white; and if it were music, a note so high it would be inaudible.

The first time I noticed the little sound come from Laïvely's throat, I didn't pay it much attention.

My sister had been gone for a few weeks, two or three months at the most. Lisa had rediscovered her taste for laughter and the little joys that day-to-day life could bring, and the tones of my world had regained the gentle pallor that they had lost months earlier.

At times, our harmony was such that you'd be for-given for believing we had always lived like this: the father, bearded, somewhat grumpy but with laughter in his eyes; the little girl, reminiscent of a young fawn, precariously balanced between the world in which she was a child and the one in which she would become a woman; and the strange robot, who had become more indispensable than any pet with a beating heart and a wet nose.

Laïvely, in a way, not only had Liv's voice, but she also played a part in our lives: she advised us, she warned us, she watched over us with kindness and tenderness, her heat sensors not letting many of our comings and goings slip by. If Lisa's hair hadn't been brushed before leaving for school, she would intervene in the hallway with a: *'One does not leave the house without clean hands and teeth, combed hair and neat clothes, young girl,'* recited in the style of an old, crabby teacher, a character Liv imitated well. Lisa would then turn around, grumbling as she stomped back up the stairs to the bathroom, sticking her tongue out at Laïvely as she passed her, who would then throw back a very proper, English *'lovely'*. These lines, which became ritual, marked every morning of the week, and Lisa took great pleasure in not brushing her hair before going downstairs. Laïvely then, was never mistaken in her algorithmic prognosis: there was a ninety-eight-percent chance that a child who was almost a teenager would not take the time to comb her hair in the morning before going to school. The time for hours spent in the bathroom with hair-spray, perfume and make-up had not yet arrived.

As for me, if I had the bad idea of serving myself one drink too many, a disparaging 'tut' would float out of the device, and by simply closing my eyes I was able to easily envision Liv's fine fingers pushing back a lock of my hair.

The house was not yet happy or lively again, no. The atmosphere of our mews would never be returned to us. There had been too much grief, too much pain since then. That's without even contemplating our uprooting – what else could we call crossing the Channel? For me, a return to a country I didn't care about; and for my daughter, the discovery of a country she had never before set foot in. In any case, we found a new equilibrium, lulled by the Beatles and Piaf, always the Piaf that had enchanted my wife so much, and whose style she had adopted for a short while. We owed it all to my sister, of course, and, admittedly to Laïvely.

I nibble unenthusiastically at a slice of bread. Opposite me, Laïvely flickers gently. She has stopped her humming. Her presence though, still calms and soothes me.

'Do you remember, darling, the evenings, when Lisa was having her bath?'

The humming starts again. Yes, Laïvely remembers. The sound of water cascading, tumbling into the bath, my daughter's little yelps when she delicately dipped a toe in, always finding the water too hot or too cold, the laughter and the splashes. Within me, the images blur – I no longer know if they come to me from London, from our games around the plastic bath placed in the middle of the living room in which our little girl pretended to learn to swim, or from the Rabbit Hole, from those weeks when life began again. Liv and Laïvely have become one in my mind, and they are nothing but tenderness and love, care and gentleness.

I lower my head onto the wax tablecloth. And I start to cry.

London

Life could have gone on like this forever. We would have had a son. He would have been called Arthur, we'd already decided. Arthur, like the king. A character we both liked. Besides, we could never seriously have baptised our son Merlin. And yet, God only knows, a little Merlin could have been quite something. He would have excelled in physics, of course. He would have loved Harry Potter. We would have discussed it with him for hours, analysing each character, giving our opinions on our favourite, before moving on to the next volume. We would have gone to every station in the capital, searching for the platform leading to the Hogwarts Express. Of course, it was obvious that J. K. Rowling was covering her tracks – the train certainly didn't leave from King's Cross.

We would have shunned the Harry Potter Museum in favour of scouring the countryside for clues to all the places Harry had set foot. We would have commented on Hermione's attitude towards Ron. We would have sworn we'd seen Dumbledore a thousand times, a beard, crooked fingers, a gaze met in the city.

Arthur would play the piano, even better than I do. Gifted with an extraordinary musical ear, he would interpret operas without having ever read the score. *Nabucco*, perhaps, would be his favourite. Unless of course he composed music for films.

Adolescence would be turbulent, but within limits both bearable for him and us. A joint or two, getting drunk with beer, girls. Just until he fell head over heels in love. A shy redhead, a lover of horses.

Having moved to Cornwall, the couple would live a peaceful existence, only interrupted by Arthur's overseas travel, leaving for one film festival or another, jetting off to receive another award.

Lisa would have been close to him, to the point she would go to stay for long periods in his countryside dwelling, their complicity never faltering. She would be the first to see him walk, the first to teach him to ride a bike, the first to hear his secrets and his childhood dreams.

Yes, we would have had a son, and then perhaps even another child. The kind you don't expect, whose arrival comes as a surprise. That child would occupy a special place, offer the possibility of redemption, a chance to succeed with what we weren't able to with the previous children. Liv would savour that pregnancy, knowing it would be her last. She would eat pink marshmallows as she lounged across the sofa, which was becoming increasingly worn by the passage of time and the inhabitants of the house. Lisa and Arthur would no longer speak about adopting a pet. Lisa would be grown up already, revelling in this pregnancy with her mother, curious, a young woman who would be the next in our family to experience such a thing. The intimacy between them, those stories about bellies, would exclude Arthur and me a little. But we would make the best of it, go for long walks along the banks of the Thames and talk, 'man to man'.

It wouldn't matter if it were a boy or a girl. Who cares about those digressions.

Even if this was how I saw our future, as I bent over my piano inventing new melodies that tasted of raspberry and were the colour of peach, I never spoke about it with Liv. She probably had her own dreams. But I liked to think that we shared that one, and that only the modesty that the strongest feelings come enveloped in prevented us from discussing it in person.

Yes, life could have gone on like that. Behind the windows of our house, the small glass panes, we would have been happy until the end of time.

I got the cupboard door to the face again.

Yesterday, I ended up downing a glass of whisky before lunch. Something I haven't done for a while. The drink burnt my throat, brought tears to my eyes, made me cough. Its warmth then spread through me, a warmth that was familiar and demonic at the same time. I shuddered. Then smiled.

I was propped up at the sink. The cupboard door crashed into my face. Less violently than the first time, but all the same.

I let out a cry of pain, which seemed to be echoed by an evil sneer. Without wasting time assessing the damage, I set off in search of Laïvely. What was going on with her?

She blinked composedly on my bedside table, innocence personified. To hell with electronics. I glared at her, threatened to pull out all those little coloured wires that made her an awful being, then left the room, violently slamming the door behind me.

In the bathroom, the mirror reflected a less than unflattering image of me. Unshaven, my scarf dishevelled, my nose once again crooked and red. A real caricature of a drunkard's honker. Worthy of an appearance in the satirical newspapers of the inter-war period. There was a little tune on the accordion to accompany it all, and the scent of roasted chestnuts mingled with that of the murky waters of the Ourcq canal. Everything was black and white.

I laughed sourly. It was like a scene from *Hôtel du Nord*, I could hear Arletty's unhinged voice, '*atmosphère, est-ce que j'ai une gueule d'atmosphère?*' If so, the atmosphere was pathetic – it stunk of cat piss with a hint of brussels sprouts.

I slathered myself in arnica tincture, then, sitting on the edge of the bath, I attempted to put my ideas in order, still clouded by the alcohol and the blow I had received.

I closed my eyes in order to be able to concentrate better, but it did nothing but make me feel like I was on a raft in the middle of the Atlantic Ocean. I opened them again, the room slowly spun around me. As long as I didn't focus on anything for too long, the spinning was manageable. A wave of exhaustion swept over me, and overcome by irrepressible yawns, I ended up back in bed.

I woke up to the sound of Babette and Téo talking in the kitchen. It was almost night. I had been absent from the world for a good part of the day.

So, I put off for tomorrow my desire to understand and overcome what was happening with me, within me.

Tomorrow is today.

Spring has finally decided to fully express itself. The birds are chirping in the now embellished garden. Two turtle-doves coo, perched on the guttering. The air is warm, the light is vibrant. Paris is decked out in its most exquisite finery. But I don't care. Locked in my office, the shutters down, I observe Laïvely. When had it all started? Was it when I put her together, trying to reproduce the notes of Liv's voice as precisely as possible? Was it when I cut that red wire a little too short? Or was it when I tapered the green? Was it when those same wires were thought of, designed, created, somewhere in China, or elsewhere? What would David say about all of this?

But perhaps I am the problem. Strange associations have always formed in my brain, and were only ever controllable, finally, when I lived in London, with Liv. Is this the first time that I've given the objects that surround me gifts they are far from able to possess? Is this parallel universe my downfall, or, on the contrary, my salvation? Does my equilibrium come from my belief in their talents, or is this the definitive proof that I am losing my mind?

It's nothing to do with Laïvely, nor me, I suddenly decide. But facts. Real, concrete facts. I have not invented anything. Liv's death. The move. The arrival of Babette and Téo. And Laïvely's mood swings. Those evil laughs really came from her, the cupboard doors truly slammed into my face. There's no way I'd ever have been mad enough to slam them into my own face. Never.

So?

There was the fall down the stairs when I left Laïvely in the garage. Then the wardrobe door, the evening Babette and I went out to dinner. And the kitchen cupboards, twice.

If Laïvely is trying to tell me something, what could it be? If she were jealous of Babette, she would have expressed her discontent earlier. Right? Could she have done things without me realising? Could I have missed other signs?

I rack my brain, my eyebrows furrowed.

Laïvely lets out a little pearly giggle. 'Oh, yes,' she seems to say, 'there have been signs. But no one is as deaf as someone who refuses to listen.'

Suddenly, a tune rises in the room. Laïvely is whistling. And then it comes back to me. Of course, there were signs. How could I have been so blind? Or reckless enough to ignore them?

London

I got back early from a work trip to Scotland. I'd been invited to the University of Glasgow to speak about my career, my journey. I'd given the usual speech – a nice little story about the self-made man. Nothing about my unique associations, which, however, perfectly explained my creations. They belonged only to me. As a child they had cut me off from others, and because I didn't want to relive the ostracisation that foreignness sometimes provokes from fellow human beings, I stuck to clichés and truisms, and everyone was happy that way.

And then I went home early. For some reason a gala dinner had been cancelled, so I took the opportunity to catch the earlier plane.

When I walked through the door to the house, only silence welcomed me. Lisa was sleeping at a friend's house. Liv must have been at her yoga class. I hadn't warned her that I was coming back early – I wanted to surprise her. In my travel bag, a reproduction of a letter from Mary Stuart to Elizabeth I, her cousin, was waiting to be gifted and framed. Liv had a near cult-like admiration for Mary Stuart. She had particularly liked the biography that Stefan Zweig had written about her; it was one of the many books that had fuelled her passion. The episode in the queen's life that fascinated her most was her escape from a lost island, where an unenviable fate awaited her. She imagined her manipulating the guards, Mary's feigned, or perhaps real, love for her jailor and saviour. Liv pictured her jumping from the boat onto the banks and setting off on horseback in frenzied flight. The romance tinged with violence nourished something within her that made her cheeks flush.

I placed the reproduction in the pram, and went to serve myself a gin and tonic. Night had fallen over the city, but I didn't bother to turn on the lights. I liked to stay in that half-darkness, making out the shapes of the living room that was existing calmly around me. Dust, cypresses, Mirabelle plums, wilted roses. All accompanied by the ticking of an old pendulum.

I closed my eyes, letting the smell of the gin rise into my nostrils, listening to my even breath fill the room, happy and tired at the same time.

I must have dozed off for a moment. It was only when I heard the noise of Liv's footsteps on the stairs, the sound of her voice, that I woke up with a start.

She was cooing. Her mobile phone glued to her ear,

her voice had those intonations that only I had ever known, intonations of someone in love. A lilting, charming babble. Mimosa perfumed with mascarpone. But this time it wasn't addressed to me.

I hesitated for a while about what to do. Should I cough to indicate my presence? Flick on the light on the coffee table? Or hope that she would go up to our bedroom without switching the lights on, without noticing my travel bag at the foot of the pram, the bottle of gin on the kitchen side, the tonic that I hadn't bothered to put back in the fridge, now humid with condensation?

She walked past without noticing me, immersed in her conversation. A little throaty giggle escaped from her every now and then. I took care not to focus on the words, but only on their music, their scent, their colour. They all spoke of love. But Liv was not addressing them to me, those signs of tenderness, those declarations of intimacy.

I listened to her attend to her nocturnal habits. The bathroom, the water running in the sink. The flush of the toilet. The jingling of the ceiling light being switched off. The creak of the bed. A sigh of contentment. The sound of the sheets being crumpled to find the most comfortable position. A yawn. Then nothing else.

I remained on the sofa, motionless, I even wondered if I was still breathing. I was no longer thinking of anything. I was empty. Hollow, even.

I don't know how long I spent like that. What did it matter?

In the morning, Liv discovered me dozing on the sofa. She woke me up with a kiss, with a laugh. I told her that I'd got back late, that I hadn't wanted to disturb her sleep. She called me a nincompoop, a big twit, words she liked the sound of, words she used with such tenderness that it made my heart ache each and every time.

For a brief moment I thought that everything was normal, that nothing had happened, that I had dreamt about her coming back. It was often the case that I distorted reality when I was really caught up in a composition, when I was searching for the right note. In times like that, reality would fade into the background and it would always take me a long time to find my feet again. I could have let myself sink into this lie if Liv hadn't made a quick movement towards her phone. She snatched it up, stuffed it into her pocket and glanced over her shoulder at me, as if to assure herself that I hadn't noticed her sleight-of-hand. In seeing my eyes on her, she blushed, smiled, but couldn't go as far as to extinguish the flicker of concealment that I read in the blue of her irises, a blue that was normally so clear and which, suddenly, seemed to contain abyssal, unexplored depths.

I got up to bury my face in her neck, as much to avoid her gaze as to find her scent.

She left half an hour later after one last kiss, leaving me to my doubts, my fears, my questions, and my rage.

The very first time Babette slept in the house, I had a strange dream.

We'd gone for dinner at the Chinese restaurant before, naturally, heading back to the Rabbit Hole. We'd been seeing each other for a few weeks, and our story was finding its rhythm, a little hesitantly, a little wobbly, but imbibed with tenderness. We had already shared some coffees, two or three dinners, as many innocent kisses. Things seemed to be unfurling naturally. But the first time my lips met hers I hadn't experienced a racing heart, sweaty hands, I hadn't even felt dizzy. The day it happened, I'd once again been the last person to leave the swimming pool, and we ended up walking at the same pace towards the metro station. Taking this little journey together had almost become a habit. I don't know why, but that day, at the moment we were about to say goodbye to each other, it felt completely natural to me to lean in towards her. She had bored her eyes into mine. In them I read a questioning, desire, and a certain form of surrender. I'm not sure what she discovered in mine.

Our lips met. Hers were full, firm – they tasted of bleach and a hint of something else that it took me months to identify. Cardamom.

Our kiss was brief, and Babette then turned away, tumbled down the stairs and was swallowed up by the mouth of the metro. I returned to the Rabbit Hole without thinking of anything, without dreaming about the future, my pulse steady. In spite of everything, I was content, if not happy.

The first time that Babette stayed over at the Rabbit Hole, we had already slept together. I have no precise memory of our first encounter, and in no way am I looking to try to explain it. It just happened. I do know, however, that I immediately loved the curves of her hips, the texture of her skin, the contours of her buttocks, the heat of her breath. She exuded a surprising sense of life. And she gave me a strange, welcome sense of life too.

After making love, she nestled up to me. Her tummy fit snugly against mine, her arms wrapped around me as if she were clinging onto a buoy. I caressed her back with a distracted hand, savouring the feel of her skin, fulfilled. Laïvely was softly playing an old Ben Harper album. Babette kissed my neck, at the border of my beard, laughing at her nostrils being tickled. I smiled. And we fell asleep.

In the night, I had that strange dream. We were, Liv and I, in Hyde Park, having a picnic. It was a beautiful June day, like only London knew how to offer. Lisa was playing a little further away – she had made friends. Liv, for once, was immersed in a contemporary novel. I couldn't make out the title on the cover, though I was convinced I had already read it. A robin sang not too far away. A cloud briefly eclipsed the sun, and Liv pushed her sunglasses onto her head. I stroked the grass, counted the blades, observed the insects that carried out their laborious life among them. I was lulled by the laughter and cries of the children around me, and the pull to have a siesta was pressing. I closed my eyes. When I opened them, Hyde Park and Liv had disappeared. Lisa no longer existed. I was alone in a deserted cemetery. Lying in a coffin, my hands crossed over my heart, my eyes fixed on a sky without stars, I contemplated the immense emptiness of a time that did not belong to me. I was cursèd, I had sold my soul to the devil in order to be the first to find eternal rest in the earth, as Christian tradition dictated. I was dead, well and truly dead. And no one was there to cry for me. I closed my eyes again. When I opened them, a woman was at my side. A stranger. She smiled at me as she caressed my cheek and whispered to me, but I didn't understand the words that crossed her lips.

My erection embarrassed me, it was indecent. But the woman stroked my sex before climbing on top of me. I felt her without feeling her, I loved her without loving her, I experienced pleasure without finishing. She arched her back, carried away by the orgasm, but my sex remained hard and firm, a flint that sliced through her insides, that stabbed her. The blood started to run down her thighs, the features of her face now winced with pain, and I watched helplessly as she moved towards death, murdered, my member the most unreasonable weapon to exist.

Babette let out a last cry of pleasure and suddenly I found myself in my bed, she arching on top of me, my sex palpitating within her. Fragments of the dream were still stuck to my skin, I had the taste of earth in my mouth, a bell was ringing in my ears, I smelt sulphur and incense. My pleasure was so powerful I thought I was going to die.

Babette let herself fall onto my torso, her heart violently beating against me. It was those beats that dragged me back into the present, to my bedroom, to this woman, to our night.

She gave me a long, tender kiss, and my hand lost itself in her blonde curls, my fingers intertwining with the hairs that I gripped like a fragile lifeline, the only salvation from a certain drowning.

The next day, at breakfast, the dream had left me for good. Laïvely sang out old Eddy Mitchell tunes, something Liv had never done. For the first time, that aluminium tube was nothing but a functional object, a home assistant that was a little more elaborate than others. Babette nattered as she sipped her coffee, her voice sounding out over the music. I had the strange feeling of watching over that scene as a spectator, but at the same time, I also had the feeling that I had never in my life been so present, so in the moment, as if nothing else would ever happen, as if for eternity I would stay there, at that table, face to face with that woman, listening to that crooner's voice playing out in the background on a spring morning.

Then a robin began to sing, and Laïvely tutted before responding with a joyful trill. Was there the slightest dissonance over that breakfast that I should have been able to identify? Am I the instrument of Babette's demise? Am I symbolically killing her? By projecting my sentiments and resentments onto Laïvely, am I absolving myself of any responsibility for the events of previous months? Is this electronic thing nothing but a receptacle for my wandering moods? Or is she gifted with what might be called a conscience? Does she feel love, jealousy, pain? Does she suffer? Does she see my life with another as hollow revenge for having been deceived by the one whose voice she has?

I am left with only one certainty: I am losing myself.

London

I truly believed I had dreamt the scene that had played out upon my return home. Sometimes I'd have blackouts. They normally happened when I remained focused on myself for too long, searching for a note that escaped me, for a taste whose name was on the tip of my tongue, for a scent that tickled my nostrils. I would then be spared these blackouts for long periods of time, sometimes years, for them only to come back again, especially after changes of place, habits, or after an emotional shock. They were all-consuming during my childhood but had completely abandoned me in adolescence, only to come back to haunt me at the start of my adult life, notably after meaningless nights with one conquest or another. After I had started living with Liv, I'd rarely had to deal with a blackout. I could only think of a handful of times that it had happened. The last was after the birth of Lisa. The turmoil that I felt at seeing her tiny body stuck against that of her mother's, a mammal already in search of a breast, propelled me into another dimension. I was there but not there; it was my story, and yet it was not. That woman who had just brought life into the world was a stranger to me. That child's life did not concern me. Camera, camera man, actor, and director – I filled all the roles at once.

I would be hard pressed to say exactly how long I had stayed there, outside of my body, my life, before reintegrating with my skin. The experience was violent, profoundly destabilising.

And the trip to Edinburgh, though it didn't quite have that kind of power, was nonetheless one of those circumstances. I had had three intense days between my conference, two meetings with producers about working on the music for a new theatre piece, dinners, networking, heavy meals, whisky and wine. Perhaps I needed, on my return, to retreat inside myself, to penetrate the internal space where dreams and reality became one, where all the hermetic boundaries between them were broken down.

After overhearing that phone call, I observed Liv more, a little more closely. She seemed largely unaffected. I did notice the appearance of a new wrinkle at the corner of her mouth, a light varicose vein at the fold of her knee. Her voice, too, had become ever so slightly deeper. She sung a little less, and suddenly preferred Souchon to Piaf or Barbara.

'Londres sur Tamise' was her favourite – she hummed it all the time. Since when?

In studying my wife like that, I realised that I had not looked at her in such a way for a long time. I thought we had been walking hand in hand towards a common goal, but maybe we had contented ourselves with simply walking side by side, and not always at the same pace.

I decided to seduce her again. Because while I was certainly paying less attention to her, she was doing the same to me. We would bump into one another in bed, or in the kitchen when we were preparing a meal – and elsewhere too – but without noting anything more than the other person's presence. Sometimes we even moved around each other, as we did with the pram – which seemed to have a life of its own and was capable of getting in the way at the least opportune moments.

So, I decided to take Liv away to Oxford for the weekend. Just the two of us. I organised it all without telling her. Lisa went to stay with Henry, who was in on the plan. On the Friday evening, I went to wait outside the theatre where Liv was working at the time so I could whisk her away to the train station and to Oxford.

She walked out of the door with a group of young

make-up artists, all chattering away. A man, the only one, was part of the group. He was a handsome guy in his fifties, a charming smile, elegant. He was holding Liv by the arm, a sign of obvious complicity.

I didn't remember her ever telling me about him. I had no idea who he could be. The director? An actor? The owner of the theatre?

They quickly took leave of the others and then rushed off down the pavement together. I didn't have time to get closer, to shout my wife's name, to let her see me, and instead stayed there, frozen, indecisive. Should I follow them? Run after them and question Liv? If that man was her lover, what would she think of my intrusion? If I followed her, it meant I didn't trust her. If he wasn't her lover, she would come to the same conclusion. It was too late now to surprise her with my train tickets, our suitcases, my loving gaze.

I hung around for a while, before going back to the house. All I had to do was wait there. We could get the next train, nothing was lost – the weekend had only just begun.

But when I came out of the underground, a message was waiting for me on my phone's voicemail. Liv excused herself, she would be getting back late, rehearsals were going on longer than expected, she was sorry.

Everything seemed vulgar to me, petit bourgeois even. It was the perfect setup for a boulevard play, with its slightly crude humour and easy-to-see-through misunderstandings. So, I still refused to believe that she was cheating on me. That our relationship was nothing but a parody of love, that it had not been able to escape clichés. That she sang in someone else's shower. That she caressed someone else's body with the same tenderness she caressed mine.

I wandered aimlessly around the neighbourhood for a long time, walking away from the house only to wander aimlessly back towards it. I had not responded to her message. She had not tried to get back in touch with me.

At eleven o'clock, exhausted, lost, I finally got on the last train to Oxford.

Babette and Téo left yesterday. We made out we believed it was all roses, happy, sweet, nice. Keep an eye on the tides! Watch out for the waves! Make sure the seafood is fresh! I had warned. Get some rest! Relax! Go out, have fun! And repair the garage door if you have time, she prompted with a complicit wink. I nodded, said goodbye to them with a last wave of the hand as they stepped out of the door, weighed down with their bags. And I went back inside the empty house.

Lisa was at a friend's for a few days. Nothing broke the silence. Not even a sigh from Laïvely.

She was sitting on the sideboard in the hallway, her indicator light green. Yet she didn't make a sound. Nothing. As if dead or mummified.

I watched her for a while. My mind empty. I didn't even think of the hundreds of hours it had taken me to assemble her, nor of the search for the perfect sound to gift her with. I had forgotten David's speech, the colours of the wires, the bluish sparks that flashed before my eyes the moment I connected two together, the taste of orange marmalade that then prickled my tongue. My mind seemed to have erased the happy memories, her capacity to turn up the thermostat in the bathroom before Lisa jumped into the bath, her recommendations for cooking the perfect al dente pasta that would be ready at exactly the same time as the sauce bubbling away in the pan, her musical taste, which ranged from Cyndi Lauper to Mozart, by way of Gershwin and Pearl Jam, tales from across the whole world that she whispered into my daughter's ear to send her off to sleep, her sagacity when it came to choosing between two TV programmes. I had removed from my mind the way in which she had taught Lisa to play chess, how she had repeated her Spanish lessons and kept her away from anything on the internet that wasn't age appropriate. It was as if the nights spent with her, listening to her softly hum Anne Sylvestre, which reminded me of my own childhood, or Balavoine, the singer of my adolescence, had never existed.

In that moment, right then, in the hallway, where darkness had finally taken over, strange, worrying shadows materialising around the furniture, even the sound of the triangle eluded me. I was an empty shell, a being of flesh and blood, with arms and legs, but nothing else, nothing other than skin and bone, a skeleton, nerves, muscles. All sensibility had abandoned me, all desire, all intention. All conscience.

I don't know how long I spent there plunged in that trance-like state, leaving the darkness to eat away at the little light that remained of the day.

Suddenly, Laïvely's light seemed to come back to life, as if she too had just woken from a long sleep. It flickered gently. Emerald then amazonite.

Hypnotised, I followed the transitions from one colour to another, carried away by a strange feeling of well-being, it was like recalling a childhood memory of strawberry and sea-salt ice cream to the tune of 'A Sailor Went to Sea'. I think I started humming softly, all whilst salivating at the thought of that ice cream.

Laïvely continued to silently diffuse those soothing lights. I swayed gently back and forth, without taking my eyes off her.

And then, nothing.

This morning I open my eyes in my bed. My bed and not my bed. I recognise everything without recognising anything. The sailor still hasn't sailed away. He is in the port awaiting his grand departure. A child devours him with his eyes as he laps up a two-scoop cone.

The music is louder in my skull. The flavours stronger. The colours vivid.

I close my eyelids again.

London

I got back from Oxford after a gloomy weekend spent in the bed of the hotel room that I had reserved for us. It was too big for me alone, the room too romantic, the city too lively. I had not switched my phone back on – Henry knew where we had gone if there was the slightest problem with Lisa. But I was confident there wouldn't be, there never was with her. He would have told her tales of indigenous people, read her poems in Greek, the sounds of which she particularly loved, made her listen to the bagpipes, and stuffed her with toast slathered in peanut butter, raspberry jam and quince jelly. She would have felt a little nauseous, but not too much, and she would have fallen asleep clutching Paddington, whom she loved dearly to her chest.

As for Liv, if she had left me messages, I wasn't ready to listen to them. All I wanted was to hear her bell-like laughter, taste the crumbs from scones on her lips, run my hand over her hips before closing my eyes. I had no desire to discover the sound of her voice in a lie – her voice that had whispered words of love to me in a language that belonged only to us, that had told me of her crazy days, that had questioned me about one of my latest creations. I oscillated between anger, rage even, and despair, fear of being cheated on, and fear of being right. Huge red clouds gathered in front of my eyes; the bergamot tea from the hotel made me nauseous, I was incapable of swallowing anything. Two little notes haunted me, they resonated like an angry metronome. Their tick-tock chanted the hours, oblivious to any rhythm other than their own.

On Sunday afternoon, I boarded the train beneath a light rain that perfectly matched my mood. I felt numb, frozen to the last fingertip, alone in a way that people are rarely conscious of.

The train was rammed: enthusiastic tourists, youngsters returning to the capital after a day spent rowing or drinking in the pubs, grandparents tired after a Sunday with the family. It was all a hubbub within which I drowned in my gloom, without even trying to capture a word whose sound had particularly pleased me, to retain the perfect timbre of a voice, husky or foreign. The universe no longer had taste, no longer had colour, no longer had light. I was drained, beat, eviscerated.

The house was empty. No sign of Liv. I roamed from

one room to the other, searching for hints, signs, clues. Had she slept here during my absence? Had she even realised I'd left? Yes, of course she had.

I imagined her getting back later that Friday evening. She would have put the key in the door as discreetly as possible, wincing at hearing the lock scrape. Then, on her tiptoes, she would have gone into the living room. In the shadows, her foot would have collided with the pram. She would have bit her lip to hold in her cry, then, limping slightly, she would have entered the kitchen to drink a final glass of water. From the quality of the silence, would she have guessed she was alone? Maybe. Now taking fewer precautions, she would have made her way up the stairs to find the bedrooms empty. The absence of Lisa, in particular, would have worried her. Had I taken her to hospital? Was she ill? Injured?

My wife would then have tried to contact me, without success. Then she would have tried Henry's number, despite the late hour. He would have been surprised to hear from her. Were we alright? She, in turn, would have been speechless. No, she wasn't with me, she had just got back, there was no one at home. Henry would have been silent for a moment, confused, before quickly assuring her that Lisa was OK. The little girl was asleep in his guest room. As for me … With a sigh he would have spilled the beans. Oxford, the surprise, the romantic weekend. But he's not answering his phone! Lisa would have said, trying to pin the blame on me. I don't know, give him time, Henry would have responded.

She would have gone to bed, shivering between the cold sheets. Worried. What did I know? What had I realised? What to tell me? How to explain?

I refused to allow myself to go any further, to come up with words to put in her mouth that I didn't want to find there.

I put my travel bag down next to the pram and slumped onto the sofa. I caught my breath, waiting to find the strength to call Henry and go and pick up Lisa.

But then there was a knock on the door, and I left my morose speculations to go and answer it.

I open and close my eyes.

I open and close my eyes.

I open and close my eyes.

Each time the setting is the same: white on white.

Then I close them again, and I don't know how much time has passed between two flutters of my eyelids.

Tick-tock. Tick-tock.

London

I got back from Oxford the very next morning, after a sleepless night in an outrageously romantic hotel room. I hadn't slept a wink all night. I had tossed and turned in the sheets, which smelt of vanilla-scented fabric softener. I hated that odour – too sweet, too syrupy, it made me nauseous, I wanted to throw up, but each time I rushed towards the bathroom, overwhelmed with retching, all I did was belch meaningless words to the porcelain white of the toilet. At the end of the night, I knew each and every one of its faults, I knew where the enamel had chipped away down to the exact millimetre, what needed repairing.

I was sunken, trembling, miserable. I watched Liv leaving around the corner of our mews as I was stepping into it from the other end. My footsteps matched hers.

I was no longer thinking. I was nothing but a slightly delayed robot with a wobbly gait, powered by a jumble of wires and cords, some of which had been cut.

Liv moved at a brisk pace, bouncing along the paving stones, dodging passers-by who were in less of a hurry than she was, skirting around a chair in a pub that a customer seemed to have torn from its table. She skipped along lightly; for moments, it looked like she was floating just a few centimetres from the floor. I dragged myself after her, bumping into heavily laden housewives, almost falling over the wheel of a pram, catching my jacket on the trunk of a tree.

We reached Bayswater Road, a strange cacophony in a city that had become even stranger. I saw the cars, the buses, the hawkers, the men wearing sandwich boards praising the excellence of one restaurant or another, distributing their leaflets, some already half torn. I knew that stereo speakers spat out crap tunes from the souvenir shops. But I could no longer hear anything. Nothing reached my ears other than the sound of Liv's ballet shoes; she was ten metres ahead of me, blind to anything that wasn't urging on her momentum.

I followed that woman through the crowd, that woman whose moans of pleasure I knew. I knew the taste of her tears, her skin, her saliva, I knew her scents. That woman whose cries I had heard after a nightmare, whose cries of anger after something stupid done on an exhausting day I had been witness to. That woman whose bras were mixed in with my boxers. Whom I had caressed, ran my lips over, sunk into. And she had become a stranger to me. Stranger than the day I saw her for the first time – just her back. And it was that back that she offered me now, that back that pulled me, that back that I was imperceptibly getting closer too, in the silent cacophony of an indifferent city.

We crossed Bayswater Road. In two stages.

On the central island, as we waited for the traffic lights to turn red to cross to Hyde Park, my hand brushed against her blouse.

She didn't feel a thing.

When I see nothing, I see everything. Each room in the Rabbit Hole appears to me in the most minute detail. I would be capable of describing with surgical precision the stain found at the side of the light switch in the kitchen, the stain that systematically reappears, no matter how many times we repaint the room. I would be able to describe the exact shape of the lock on the toilet door, a convoluted thing that must date back to the nineteenth century, or perhaps comes from a second-hand Art Deco dealer inspired by the previous century. I also know exactly which slat was damaged when we moved the piano from one room to another. The movers may have been professionals, but they still scuffed the wallpaper on the second floor, on the corner of the staircase. Babette had been quick to colour in the spot, using a felt-tip pen of the exact same shade as the paper, but it can't fool every-one – the repair may be perfect, but I know that there's a flaw. I also know that a little further down the hallway, on the floor, a slat has a splinter.

So, each time I close my eyes, all these imper-

fections, these wounds, these cuts, come to mind.
Sometimes, too, I take a walk through Laïvely. Now
shrunken, I'm able to study her wires, their colours,
their layout. I flush out the slightest speck of dust,
responsible, perhaps, for her mood swings. I blow, I
blow on them, hoping to chase them away, giving her
back the perfection she had in the early days. When
she took care of us. When she laughed with us, that
laugh that was a hug, a colourful, shimmering hard-
boiled sweet. But she had grown old and rusty, her
voice broke, became hoarser, the perfect replica of
Liv's when she would have her short outbursts of
anger, the dirty teapot, the folded corner of a page in
a book.

I open and close my eyes.

White, white, white.

London

I got back from Oxford the very next day.

I had slept like a log, knocked out by the champagne I had drunk alone, in the night, numbing my pain and her betrayal.

I boarded the train, a hellish hangover in tow. My atrocious burping scared off the man in the seat next to me, surely fearing that I would end up vomiting into his lap.

The journey felt endless. I was thirsty. And of course, I'd forgotten to buy a bottle of water in the train station.

I wanted to be at home, to have a shower and curl up in my bed, our bed, to sleep off the wine and the distress, to wake up feeling like a new man, a man capable of confronting his adulterous wife, a man assured of his right, legitimate in his anger. A man that could have said: 'Darling, I love you, none of it matters, forget it,' as easily as, 'Your suitcase is ready, bitch. Get out.' The kind with hair on his chest and big hands, those of a lumberjack or a butcher, for example. Yes, the kind of guy who could cut down trees or oxen in one fell swoop.

When I walked onto the mews, Liv and Lisa were leaving Henry's. I heard their chatter, hoped that they were heading to the park. I didn't want them to see me like that, a hopeless bloke who had lost all trace of his virility at the prospect of being cuckolded.

The gods were in my favour – they left the narrow street to head in the direction of Bayswater Road. I knew the route by heart, of course, I'd walked it so many times with Lisa's tiny hand between my long, fine pianist's fingers. She was particularly fond of balancing on the kerb at the edge of the pavement, pretending to be a trapeze artist suspended on an almost invisible fine wire, high up beneath the big top, performing tricks that drew shrieks of fear and admiration from the audience, frightened and excited at the idea that she could fall from up there.

But then, Lisa was not playing at being another. Except, perhaps, a pale imitation of her mother. She matched Liv's pace – Liv, who was attentive to her posture, letting her sage skirt flutter, her bust straight and upright, her chin lifted.

I followed them, and they didn't turn around. At moments, I lost them in the Saturday-afternoon crowd. They disappeared from my gaze and then a strange emptiness formed within me, a white veil cloaking everything, not a sound to be heard. The world was empty, I was walking through a polar desert, without warmth, without love, without life.

Then I saw them again, mother and daughter, happy at being together, completely oblivious to the rest of the world, absolutely oblivious to the daggers that were sinking into my heart at the image they were offering me. Then, the world became blood, crimson was the word I tasted on my lips, parched from drunkenness and the heat – crimson, a word that sounded like both a curse and a promise. Liv should have been overwhelmed, destroyed at the idea that I had figured out her betrayal. She should have been rushing to Oxford, ready to get down on her knees in front of mine, my strong lumberjack's or butcher's knees. She should have swept her hair across the floor, ripped off her shirt in atonement. Crying, cursing herself, she should have begged for my forgiveness. And coldly, like an ancient king, a god even, I would hurl at her from my lofty throne, my male honour, my virility: 'Woman, you are the door to the Devil. It is you who touched the tree of Satan, and who first violated divine law,' citing Tertullian. And then she would know that forgiveness was out of the question, so great was her sin. She would realise just how much she had lost, all for a charming smile, a gallant remark, a nicely wrapped compliment.

Overwhelmed, destroyed, she would stay lying across the floor as if mortally wounded, splayed out on the bedroom's Persian rug as I stepped over her without a last glance, leaving the vermin to its macabre fate.

We had arrived at Bayswater Road. The noise of the traffic, the laughter, the conversations, the music that escaped from the shops for tourists drilled into my ears. I had the feeling that I was going blind, that I was lost in an era that wasn't mine, in a tale in which I did not have a role.

The elegant fifty-something stepped forwards. Liv let out a little cry of pleasure that drowned out all the sounds of the city. She left a light peck on the cheek of the man, presented our daughter to him, who, timid, hid behind her mother's legs. All three advanced towards the pedestrian crossing. The lights for the cars were green. They sensibly waited to cross.

If Liv had been a little more attentive, she would have felt my whisper on her neck. Felt my hand on her lower back.

But Liv was no longer wise to my presence. She had gone too far.

I open and close my eyes.

I open and close my eyes.

I open and close my eyes.

Each time the setting is the same: white on white.

Then, I close them again, and I don't know how much time has passed between two flutters of my eyelids.

Vermillion, carmine, cherry, garnet, poppy, currant, amaranth, burgundy, crimson.

Kaki, pistachio, olive, sage, forest, avocado, grass, emerald.

Mustard, amber, canary, banana, buttercup, hyacinth, butter, duck.

Azure, indigo, navy, cerulean, sky, marine, turquoise, cornflower.

And then, white, white, white. Polar.

London

But then there was a knock on the door, and I left my morose speculations to go and answer it.

Henry stared at me for a long time without uttering a word. He was haggard, ashen. I'd always seen him dressed to the nines, so his appearance was so shocking to me, I didn't even notice Lisa's absence from his side.

Without saying a word, he took me by the arms to guide me back inside to the sofa I had just taken the trouble of leaving.

Then he opened his mouth, but all I saw escape were monsters with sharp fangs and fiery eyes. Demons. I recognised Eurynome, with his long teeth, his body covered in wounds and the fox skin that only half covered him. Paimon followed him, perched on his camel, and Amdusias gave one of his secret concerts, in which the trumpets sounded out without being seen. The Duke of Hell was accompanied by Bune who, a corpse in his arms, was already delighting in having moved it without anyone noticing. There were more – others that I struggled to identify, and all of them were screeching, haranguing, looking to get the upper hand, to the point where it was impossible to hear what Henry was saying, a Henry who was now shaking me until my teeth chattered, and whom I stopped dead in his tracks when he raised his hand to me.

Suddenly the princes and the dukes of hell disappeared, as if they had never been there.

And Henry's voice finally reached me.

'Liv died as soon as she arrived at the hospital. It was too late. There was nothing they could do. I'm sorry, Stan. I'm so sorry.'

And he collapsed beside me, his body ravaged by sobs, nonsensical sounds escaping from his lips, sounds in which at times I seemed to make out the syllables that made up my daughter's name.

My eyes remained dry, staring at the white wall in front of me.

I no longer know what happened in the days that followed. I was only capable of stomaching the smallest scraps of information. Then, in the evening, like Penelope unravelling her work, I tied the threads together.

Liv had got back late, as I had imagined. She had called Henry. Gone to his. He had told her where she could find me. And she had decided to surprise me herself, taking the first train to Oxford the next day, Lisa in tow. The romantic getaway would turn into a family weekend away, the ultimate reward, love that surpassed all others. Priorities would take their place again.

How could the accident have happened? And in such an absurd way, ridiculous and unworthy of her. What had her last thoughts been? A Piaf tune? A resounding *shit*? An *as long as I don't ladder my tights*? Would it have been something trivial, or something powerful, worthy of the occasion? I will never know.

The funeral was sad and sober. I didn't try to spot among the friends that came the handsome fifty-something who she had left the theatre with just a few days before. That was no longer important.

Laila, a friend from the very beginning, had come all the way from Dorset. Stunned, she tried to console me, but her own grief was already too heavy to carry. The friend Liv did yoga with also came to say some kind words to me. I wasn't able to remember her name. I smiled a little sadly while looking down at our feet, noticing the clod of earth that was stuck to her navy-blue stiletto, wondering if I should tell her. She was pretty, well groomed, I couldn't imagine her being able to accept that something like that was possible, that something like that would happen to destroy her perfection. The more she spoke, the more that mud obsessed me. Its smell was in my nostrils, its taste in my mouth. I even heard the squelch that her foot made having sunk itself into the damp ground. Was it the earth that they would have to dig up to make room for the dead they were burying that day?

The line of condolences continued. Henry was there to support me, stood on my left. On my right, the spectral presence of Lisa.

A few weeks later, London disappeared, swallowed up by the noise of the carriages of the Eurostar grinding on the rails.

I open my eyes.

Laïvely flickers. Emerald and amazonite. My gaze remains fixed on those two tones of green, supposed to bring peace and healing to the soul.

For a time, green had been Liv's favourite colour. It went so well with the red of her hair, so red you'd have thought she was Scottish, and people even fell for it. She loved green so much that even our meals were in an infinite variety of shades. Salads, cabbage, broccoli, carrot tops, avocados, cucumbers, kiwis, watermelons, limes, soursop, olives, mint, basil, artichokes, apples, beans, peas … The list never seemed to end.

The shades on our plates had amused us. Liv had even managed to get her hand on a whole range of crockery that ranged from opaline to pistachio.

Is that why I chose to use green when I created Laïvely? Or was it simply because that was the colour that gave us permission to go, to continue, to cross, to move forwards?

The meanders that certain thoughts follow

resemble a labyrinth that Ariadne's thread could never get me out of. Green takes me back to Alice's rabbit, to the Rabbit Hole. He is not there. Only in Laïvely's whims.

I turn towards the window. The plane tree is covered in leaves. They too are green, of course. Oxygen. Respiration. Breath.

It's a nice day today, the sun is shining. For the first time in weeks, it feels like – months, maybe. I have no idea what day of the week it is. I don't know how long Babette and Téo have been away for. Twenty-four hours? Five days? I have the feeling of having completed a long and slow journey myself. I went back in time and rediscovered Liv's kisses, the sound of her laugh, so sweet and harmonious. I rediscovered our walks through London, making love in her little bedroom, playing in the pubs, and then Greenwich, Paddington, the pram, Henry, the success, the holidays, Lisa, baby babbling, the donkey's jawbone, the piano, and all the rest. Yes, all the rest. The concealments and the lies. The absences and evasive glances. The drinking. The silence, worse than the insults.

I had not heard her last scream. Nor those of the passers-by. Nor the dull thud of the bus against my wife's and daughter's bodies, the latter dragged under the wheels of the monstrous vehicle by her mother's hand. I was already somewhere else. All of that no longer concerned me.

I'm heavy with the burden of my past.

A vague scent of chlorine comes to tickle my nostrils. Babette. Yes, there's Babette too.

When had I been whole, in possession of my destiny? When I lived in London, with my wife and child? When I arrived at the Rabbit Hole? In the arms of Babette?

I no longer know where to situate my absences from the world, or my place within it. I no longer know what is dream and what is reality. Do dashing fifty-somethings seduce make-up artists backstage at the theatre? Do composers enjoy the intoxication of the monotonous melody of the swell?

I touch my nose. There's no trace of violence from the cupboard. I look down at my hands. Did they really grab Téo? Play the piano? Caress a woman's body?

I get up slowly. The floor creaks under my weight. I recognise the sound. I walk over to the bedroom door, turn the handle, and go out onto the landing. My gaze wanders up the stairs to the second floor.

Slowly, I climb them. So slowly it's as if I'm wishing never to reach the top.

I slow down even more at the last step. In front of me, the hallway, the doors.

My heart remains calm, its rhythm unchanged. A current of air comes to brush against my cheek, tenderly. I lose my breath.

I push open the first door. The double room. Lisa's. Aunt Agathe's in the past. And mine, somehow, too.

The room is filled with shadows, the shutters down. It smells humid and closed off. The dust makes my eyes itch. I blink. It's been a long time since someone was in here. Chrysanthemums, azure-white, juicy, ripe apricots.

The contours finally begin to take shape. An old, cherry-wood bed. A desk. Boxes piled up beneath a fraying blanket. Paintings turned against the wall.

Relics. A worn garnet divan. A lamp with a fringed shade.

On an old rickety dressing table with tarnished marble, something sparkles, touched by the light coming from the hallway, irresistibly attracting me.

A rose barrette.

Acknowledgements

We don't always know where the novel we have written comes from. But I know to whom I owe *Double Room*. So, thank you…

To my late grandma, Mouty. You are the one who made me love reading. And the one who brought me to London for the first time. I will never forget our trips to England, this country you admired and loved so fiercely.

To Florence, without whom *Double Room* would simply not exist.

To Laurent, for introducing me to the Mouzzaïa district, even though I grew up in Paris.

A book also exists thanks to all of those that transform a Word document into this object that you are holding in your hands…

Thank you to the whole team at Pontas Literary Agency, in particular to Anna Soler-Pont and Carla Briner. In you both I have found good listeners, and caring and attentive agents who are second to none. Love you to the moon and back!

Thank you to Orenda Books, who have given this book a life in English, making one of my craziest dreams a reality. Karen, West, Cole, Danielle, and the whole team, you're incredibly wonderful, wonderfully incredible, and great professionals. You can't imagine how moved I have been at each stage of this adventure. Thank you for your time, your energy, and your patience (I'm well aware that my English is a little rusty…). Thank you for your brilliant, luminous and mysterious cover, which I've fallen in love with!

Last but not least, thank you to Alice Banks for her work as translator. I always looked forward to your questions, sometimes even regretting that there weren't more. Our discussions and your thoroughness have taught me a lot about my own work as a translator. I couldn't have wished for a better translator than you!

Finally, thank you to you, the readers, for immersing yourselves in the Rabbit Hole and Stan's world.